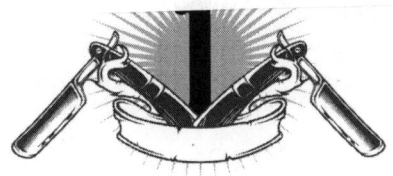

TOUCHED
BY
MAGIC

CELINE JEANJEAN

This book is a work of fiction. The characters, incidents and dialogue are drawn from the author's imagination and are not to be construed as real. Any resemblance to actual events or persons, living or dead, is coincidental.

ISBN: 9782492523236

Cover by: bonobobookcovers.com
Editing by: copybykath.com

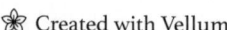 Created with Vellum

CLICK HERE TO JOIN MY NEWSLETTER

AND RECEIVE THESE FREE STORIES

Subscribe to Celine Jeanjean's newsletter and receive these
three novellas for free!
Go to:
http://celinejeanjean.com/razor-bonus

1

Nobody ever expects a girl barber, but I handle a cutthroat razor like a dream, and I can shave the hair off a bee's ass mid-flight.

I'm on my way to the barbershop, and the street is loud with the clatter of iron shutters as shops close up for the evening. It rained earlier, puddles of water reflecting the heavy lead-grey sky so they look silver. They resemble enormous coins, and it reminds me of the song "Pennies from Heaven," so I hum it to myself, enjoying the leftover dampness in the air.

I should specify, at this point, that I'm humming the Billie Holiday version, *not* the Frank Sinatra one. A girl's gotta have standards, after all.

I'm in a rundown part of Panong's Old Town, where the streets are lined with dirty tenement buildings, their long-ago white walls now streaked with black grime. A lot of the buildings are derelict, broken windowpanes gaping like missing teeth. The shops occupying the ground floor either specialise in the seedier trades—pawnshops and seriously depressing brothels—or they house specialist craftsmen who take advantage of the cheap rent found here. Which is how you can find prostitutes next door to beautiful paper lantern makers or opera headdress creators.

But the best thing about Old Town is that it's full of just the kind of nooks and crannies the Mayak—Panong's magical folk—need to exist. People in Panong cling to their traditions like Hong Kong fashionistas cling to their Gucci purses, which is why esoteric craftspeople can survive in this age of internet and smartphones and why the magical community thrives here.

I pass a huge banyan tree growing on the side of the road. It's revered—rightfully so—and the buildings retreat from around it, creating a kind of plaza around its trunk. When I say trunk, what I really mean is trunks. The tree looks more like a many-legged insect, having had centuries to send aerial roots to the ground then thicken them into yet more limbs. Once-vibrant saffron ribbons, now turned to grubby rags by time and rain, have been wrapped around the trunks. Offerings of food and incense crowd its roots and branches. The tree keeps splitting the concrete with its roots, so the road here is always in disrepair. But no one would dare suggest the tree be torn down.

I wave a greeting to the little Mayak living in the banyan tree and continue on. Only a few steps further I get the sense of someone watching me. I look around, but don't see anything or anyone. I shrug. Probably nothing, but I'll keep an eye out just to be safe.

I stop to grab some dumplings from Chanthara's stall, but he's not here today. Instead there's a kid behind the counter. Mid-twenties, the crotch of his jeans reaching for his knees (whatever happened to style?), hair that took longer to put together than the dumplings I'm about to order.

I say "kid" but he's only a few years younger than I am. Non-Touched humans always seem so young to me, like toddlers who know nothing about the world.

"Six soup dumplings, please."

The kid frowns at me. "You're not from around here."

Only an impressive amount of self-restraint stops me from rolling my eyes hard enough to give myself an injury. Mundanes always feel the need to pester me about where I'm from.

In London, it doesn't matter that my accent could rival the queen's, that I can navigate my way around the tube blindfolded, or that I know more about ale than most "true" Brits. My features are Asian, so there's always some idiot asking me where I'm *really* from—or if they're going for the prat-of-the-week award, *what* I am.

Here, in Panong, I look right, but growing up in London means my accent has a bit of a twang to it. Panongian is a tonal language, like Cantonese or Thai, and I still can't quite master the more delicate subtleties of intonations. I'm completely bilingual—I speak, read, write, think, and dream in both languages, but in Panong, if I open my mouth, I get looks and questions because I don't sound right.

That's one of the things I love best about the Mayak. Don't get me wrong, they're as prejudiced as Mundanes—probably even more so. But they couldn't care less about things like ethnicity or nationality. All human races are considered equally inferior, and as a Touched, I have the dubious privilege of being part of the dregs of magical society, relegated to the fringes. But at least no one cares about how I look or how I sound, and no one has the *slightest* bit of interest in where I'm supposed to be from.

I arch an eyebrow at the kid inside the stall and ignore his question. "My dumplings?"

He blushes. "I didn't mean anything by it, just that your accent is different." He fishes out the dumplings and places them in a cardboard container. He smiles shyly as he hands it to me. "I like your hair."

My hair's bright pink, and I'm also quite the fan of it, so I smile at the kid, deciding to forgive and forget the question about where I'm from. That's the thing about toddlers—they often stumble or say silly things. You can't hold it against them.

Eating dumplings the moment they're off the steamer is a bit like taking your chances with a piece of molten lava. The *sensible* thing to do is to wait until they've cooled down so you don't burn your mouth.

I've never been too fussed about sensible, and patience is a virtue I lack.

Which is why, moments after leaving the stall, I find myself wincing in pain from the scalding liquid bursting out of the dumpling.

"Owwww." I open my mouth to inhale cool air. The dumpling feels like it's attempting to burn a hole through my tongue. I know, I know. One day I'll learn, but for now I'm just a sucker for those explosions of savoury, porky goodness.

In spite of the dumpling distraction, I still pick up on the observer watching me. I've just turned onto the street of the barbershop, and I stop walking, pretending to fuss with my cardboard container. I carefully scan to see what I can pick up. I can't sense a magical signature, so it might be a Mundane, or it might be something able to hide itself effectively from me.

Touched humans, as a rule, aren't particularly powerful, and I'm one of the weaker ones. There are plenty of beings out there who can keep themselves hidden from my senses, so that doesn't really narrow things much.

Still, I'm not worried. I'm close enough to the barbershop that I'm squarely in Mr. Sangong's territory. That in itself will be enough to deter most of the Mayak from giving me trouble, and anyone strong enough to take on Mr. Sangong wouldn't bother with little old me any more than a black belt would feel the need to challenge a cockroach to a fight.

I know, I just compared myself to a cockroach. Before you worry about my self-esteem, that's just how a lot of the more powerful Mayak view the Touched. You get used to it, mostly because that means they leave us alone.

I reach the barbershop. Yep, I'm definitely being watched. Could be someone who wants to talk to Mr. Sangong and is feeling shy or scared. These days I take care of all the barber work while Mr. Sangong attends to other business. Mayak business that I can't know about because I'm Touched.

The barbershop technically isn't so much a shop as a space between two tenement buildings across which a front has been erected. I go through the rigmarole of unlocking the iron shutter and hold it open for a moment, partly to sense my observer, partly to give them a chance to come and accost me. They're still there, but they don't take the bait.

I wonder what this is going to be about.

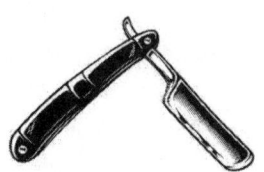

2

I slip under the shutter and let it clatter shut behind me. The shop's dark, and I lean my shoulder against the light switch. Yellow light fills the space. If I were a Mundane, all I would see is a narrow, abandoned space occupied by some mouldy cardboard boxes, a couple of rusted blue trolleys, and of course, a lot of cockroaches.

Instead, I'm greeted by a shop several times the size of the space it should be occupying. The floor is chequered black and white, gleaming under the warm light. Along the far wall is a row of four Paidar barber chairs—the real deal, from the 1930s, lovingly maintained by Mr. Sangong. In front of each chair is a mirror, a basin and tap, and a small shelf for the various shaving and hair-cutting implements.

The rest of the shop is decorated with memorabilia from Mr. Sangong's centuries as a barber. Photos of prestigious clients cover one wall, with paintings for those Mr. Sangong barbered in the days before photography. The Genghis Khan one is infused with the same magic da Vinci used with the Mona Lisa, and his golden eyes glare at me as I move around the barbershop. You get used to it.

A glass case displays three cutthroat razors from Mr. Sangong's time in Europe. The top one was used for Nikola Tesla during one of his London visits—he's Mr. Sangong's favourite client to date. The second razor was used for Louis XVI's final shave before the French Revolution took his head, and the bottom one was a gift from a fellow barber—Sweeney Todd. Now, he's one I would have liked to meet.

As I head towards the office, I check outside the shop—I can still sense my mysterious observer. I open the office door to find Timothy, a black witch's cat, curled up on the desk.

"Wake up, time to work," I tell him.

My dumplings are cool enough to eat without burning myself, so I quickly finish the last couple, chucking the cardboard container in the recycling bin. While the shop feels like stepping back into the 1920s, the office is your standard twenty-first-century fare. Desk, metal filing cabinets, swivel chair. Ugly and practical. There are no windows, and the dark teal wallpaper makes the room feel closed-in. I try to spend as little time in here as I can.

Tim does what cats do best and ignores me—nothing new there. I head over to the chairs. Sometimes he gets to work once I've gone so he can technically say he hasn't listened to me. I start stropping my favourite razor, a ten-millimetre square-pointed razor nicknamed The Lucifer. Its handle is onyx inlaid with—what else?—a little silver devil. Mr. Sangong gave it to me when he declared me ready to work without his supervision, and it shaves like a dream.

I finish stropping The Lucifer and give the black-and-white floor tiles a quick once-over. Not that I need to. The shop is so clean you could eat off the floor, and I know this because I'm the one who cleaned it last night—as I do every night. Cleaning for me is as relaxing as watching TV for most people. I like the smell of the wood polish, the faintly astringent scent of the floor cleaner, and there's nothing I hate more than coming in of an evening to find stray hairs on the white tiles.

Tim, meanwhile, still hasn't budged.

"Tim!" I call. "We'll have clients arriving soon."

"Pull the other one, treacle. Cats don't take orders from inferiors."

On top of being a witch's cat, Tim's a cockney, for his sins. Mr. Sangong picked him up during one of his many stints in London. I have no idea what Tim's age is, but he has the typical stubbornness of older magical creatures.

As a Touched, I may accept my position at the bottom of the Mayak food chain, but even I won't stand for getting attitude from a cat. "Well then, said cat should learn to get to work without me having to tell him."

No answer.

I return to the office—Tim still hasn't moved. "Your Highness better get your ass into gear, or I'll do it for you."

Tim lifts his head, angling it to show me the underside of his chin. "Scratch my chin, love."

"You should know by now that I'm a dog person." I grab him and throw him out the office door.

Tim yowls in annoyance, landing on his feet. He looks back at me over his shoulder, green eyes glaring. "You daft cow, I ain't gonna forget this."

"Glad to hear it—maybe next time you can remember to get to work without me having to throw you out of the office."

Tim gives me another look and begins to deliberately wash himself—the cat equivalent of flipping me the bird. I give a snort of laughter and leave him to his ablutions,

returning to finish setting up the chairs. Tim
insulting me, and he heads over to the lounge are

The lounge area is for clients to wait or hang out
decked out with bits and pieces from Mr. Sangong's time in
Prohibition-era Chicago. An art deco cream velvet sofa with
a black-varnished frame and three black leather club chairs,
all arranged around a low glass coffee table on brass legs.
Against the wall is the bar, stocked with a pretty decent
selection of booze—and I do say so myself, since I'm the one
who stocks it. And there's a gramophone that gives a sweeter
sound than any of the crap you'd find in an Apple shop.

One of my little tricks.

"I ain't pouring no drinks," Tim warns as he jumps up
on a black-and-gold Louis Süe armchair next to the bar.

I'm not sure why he bothers telling me that. He's never
poured a drink, and no one has ever expected him to, what
with his lack of opposable thumbs. There's no magic in the
world that can make a cat pour a decent martini, but he
likes to make that point anyway when he's in a bad mood.
Something about having the last word, I guess.

His job is to make sure the honesty bar is kept honest.
There's a jar for notes and coins on the bar. I return to my
preparations, when I sense someone about to enter. I face
the entrance. My mysterious observer?

3

Mr. Sangong enters the barbershop. "Good evening, Apiya."

To the untrained, Mundane eye, Mr. Sangong looks like any ordinary sixty-year-old man in a rather cheap grey suit. His face is unremarkable, neither particularly attractive, nor memorably ugly. His hair is grey, his features leaning a little towards Chinese, hinting at Chinese ancestry, like so many in Panong. We've had a steady stream of Chinese immigrants over the centuries, and Panong isn't a very big island. Almost every Panongian can point to some Chinese ancestry.

Mr. Sangong appears so ordinary, even I have to focus to be able to detect the magic around him, and unless I work hard at it, I can't recognise him before he enters the barbershop.

That's how you can tell a truly old Mayak from a young one—the young ones are sloppy and leak magic every-where. And they're generally still vain enough to choose attractive or distinctive glamours. Obviously the shape-shifters only have one human appearance, and they can't change it.

Mr. Sangong took me in as a protégée back when I first arrived in Panong. He taught me to navigate Panong's magical underbelly, gave me a job, and even tried to help grow my magic. But it's so weak, that was a bit of a waste of everyone's time. He never told me as much—Mr. Sangong is unfailingly polite. He just gradually stopped training me.

I don't mind—I can't help having weak magic, any more than I can help the way I look. And Mr. Sangong has never once spoken to me or treated me like an inferior.

"Bloody tart threw me out the office," Tim complains, jumping atop a cabinet so he's level with Mr. Sangong's arm.

Mr. Sangong scratches his head distractedly.

"I picked up on someone watching me as I came in," I say.

"Hmm. Nothing dangerous." He disappears into the office and closes the door.

A man in his thirties enters the barbershop, wearing a sharp suit, patent leather shoes, and an open-collared shirt.

"Hi, Ari," I greet him. Not my observer—I know Ari well enough to recognise his signature from a distance, and anyway, a kitsune has better things to do with his time than to spy on me.

"Hey, Apiya, how's it going?" Ari breaks into a smile. His glamour isn't a particularly handsome man, but what he lacks in perfection of features, he more than makes up in charm. I had quite the crush on him when I first met him— it's the way he smiles.

I usher him to one of the chairs. "The usual?"

Ari has never let me see his fox form, and my magic is insufficient to sense beyond his glamour to the number of tails he possesses. Kitsunes grow one for every hundred years they've been alive. Ari's too smooth and controlled to be young.

Now, you're probably wondering what a Japanese magical creature is doing in Panong. The thing is, kitsunes existed long before the concept of Japan was even a gleam in any Mundane's eye. The Mayak have always moved around, but some of them have areas they favour and spend more time in.

Kitsunes, for some reason, quite liked Japan back in the day, which meant Mundanes sometimes picked up on them, and thus the Mundane myths were born. But in truth, for the Mayak, countries and nationalities are the same as religions—hallucinations invented and shared by the Mundanes.

The only borders they recognise are defined by mountains, water, or magic. There's a large Mayak-recognised border between the Asian and European territories, which is why the Asian Mayak remain in Asia, and the European fae stay in Europe. There is some inter-territory travel, of course, but I hear it's a complicated affair that makes Mundane diplomacy look like child's play.

As for religions, there's no such thing. There is only magic, the beings made of it, and the beings touched by it. So a kitsune is no more Japanese than Kali is a Hindu goddess. Kali is Kali. Kitsunes are kitsunes, and anything else is a Mundane fairy tale.

I grab a black waxed-cotton cape, snap it smartly, and sweep it around Ari's neck, the cape flaring out like the swing of a fifties skirt. Then I get a fresh hot towel, shake it out, and wrap it around his face. I re-strop The Lucifer while I wait for the heat to open his pores. The Lucifer is already sharp enough to work with, but I find clients like to hear the sound of steel against leather while they relax with a towel on their face.

A werecat comes in while I'm in the middle of the shave. His human form is mid-to-late thirties and is broader than most cats' human form. He wears heavy boots, jeans, and a black T-shirt that does wonders for his muscled chest. I guess he must shift into one of the larger cats—tiger or leopard. I hope it's a tiger.

"Take a seat. I'll be right with you."

The werecat goes to the lounge area and inspects the bar.

"You better cough up, sunshine," Tim mutters from his chair.

The werecat snorts with laughter. You have to give it to Tim—it takes guts to give attitude to a creature that can swallow you in a couple mouthfuls. But that's cats for you—tiny animals with enough arrogance to think they rule the world.

I turn my attention back to Ari's shave, gently scraping the cutthroat razor against the underside of his jaw, enjoying the faint rasp of the blade against his skin.

"Anyone mind if I put some Ellington on?" the werecat asks, fingering one of the records beneath the gramophone.

I finish Ari's shave to the Duke's smooth tones, then it's time to attack the werecat. Barbering a were—whether wolf or cat—is akin to trimming a hedge. At first there's no room for subtlety. You've just got to hack through the growth. Even an Asian were—they're a bit less hairy than their European counterparts, but that's not saying much. With enough patience and determination, though, you can do a little delicate work at the end.

Of course it only lasts until the next shift, but I have a

reputation to uphold, and I like my clients to leave the shop looking as sharp as my razors.

Ari and the werecat both decide to stay with us for a bit, drinking whiskey and listening to music. I always like it when clients hang around—the sound of conversation and ice cubes in tumblers on top of the music. It gives the shop a kind of speakeasy feel. Sometimes I like to pretend we're back in the roaring twenties. Obviously, I'm a glaring anachronism in the picture, with my combat boots and ripped fishnets.

Okay, I'm sure you think I'm a bit of hypocrite for dissing the drop-crotch trousers of the kid at the dumpling stall, given how I dress. What can I say? I've got double standards, and I like men who dress sharp just as much as I like to dress grungy. Which of course ensures that the sharply dressed men don't find me appealing. A shrink would call it self-sabotage that keeps me permanently single. I call it being complex and happily single.

It's all about perspective.

Mr. Sangong comes out of the office, still looking preoccupied. "I'm going to need to leave for the night."

"Anything I can help with?" I ask, probably too eagerly.

I know Mr. Sangong doesn't like it when I pester him to take me deeper into Mayak society, but sometimes it's frustrating. There's a whole world just out of my reach, and it would be open to me if only Mr. Sangong would allow it. But he keeps telling me that it's too dangerous for me, even though I handle myself just fine with our clients.

Of course that's mostly—entirely—because the barbershop is Mr. Sangong's turf, so his magic protects me. But still.

Mr. Sangong gives me a penetrating look. That's as close

as he ever gets to showing disapproval. "No, thank you, Apiya."

I look away, knowing I've been chastised. I sigh as he walks out. I'm grateful to him and the place he's given me in the magical world of Panong. I am. On my own, I probably would never have managed it, or at least not so well. But sometimes I wish he'd relax his rules a bit.

After the werecat, I have a pre-booked appointment with a garuda who likes to see me in his natural form. Garudas have the body of a man and the head of an eagle, which makes barbering tricky. But barbering to the supernatural means being able to deal with any form, magical or human. I pull out the magical razors and start stropping. One of them in particular gives such precision to movements, Mr. Sangong trained me until I could actually shave a bee's ass mid-flight without killing it.

Did you think I was bragging earlier?

I'm almost done stropping the smallest of my razors, the one I use for real precision work, when I sense a new arrival. This time I recognise my observer. I watch the entrance, curious.

4

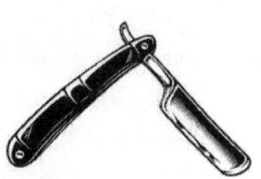

A pretty couple walks into the barbershop, decked out like they just stepped out of the pages of a lifestyle magazine. Expensive designer clothes, sleek, artfully arranged hair, and manicured nails. And that's just the guy.

They aren't shifters—I can sense that much—so they have to be glamours. Other than that, though, I'm at a loss. I haven't sensed their kind before.

Unfortunately, it's supremely rude to ask a Mayak what they are, so I'm going to have to sit on my curiosity.

The girl sweeps a look over the barbershop, clutching her cross-body handbag with both hands. Her beau stands protectively next to her. Something about their manner suggests that they're young—my money would be on less than a hundred.

"Hello, and welcome," I call. "I'm just finishing up with a client, but I'll be with you as soon as I can." I gesture at the lounge area.

"Th-thank you," the girl stammers, not meeting my eye.

She scurries away from me as if I'm a big bad wolf who's about to eat her.

Her beau follows.

I watch them, a tad bemused. I've been told that I can be intimidating at times, which is just ridiculous. I'm nice as pie, me. I get why I sometimes freak out some of the more conservative Mundanes, though—the pink hair, biker boots, and tattoos have certain connotations. But really that's just a reflection of how narrow-minded people can be, and how much they like to stereotype.

The Mayak aren't narrow-minded about appearances, and none of them should be scared of me. Something must have gotten the couple so spooked they're behaving like a couple of meek little Mundanes.

I go back to my garuda and finish tending to his feathers, glancing back at the couple from time to time. She's folded herself into one of the chairs, still clutching her bag, eyes wide. He's standing behind her, a protective hand on the back of the chair, and he's sweating.

The werecat tries drawing them into the conversation with the kitsune, but he quickly loses interest when they answer in tense monosyllables.

They're real scared, all right.

Interesting.

I don't prolong their ordeal, finishing up with the garuda, who decides not to stay for a drink. Shame. I've outdone myself, and he's looking pretty fine.

Once he's gone, I usher the couple to the middle Paidar chair, a little annoyed that I don't have a chance to clean up after the garuda. Traces of lather in the basin tug at my attention.

I put up a wall of silence so we are cocooned in quiet, the music and conversation faint and muffled, as if at a distance.

Before you start thinking my magic is impressive, I can't do this outside of the barbershop. So long as I'm on Mr. Sangong's turf, my magic feeds off his. It helps a lot with clients taking me seriously.

"What can I do for you?" I ask the girl.

Her lower lip starts to tremble, and her beau puts an arm around her. He glances at the lounge area.

"Do you need more privacy than silence?" I ask him.

They both nod.

I put up a second wall, and the light dims, turning the barbershop dark, as if we're seeing it through black gauze, although the three of us are still perfectly visible.

"So?" I ask them.

The girl's face twists. "We need... we need... something taken out of Panong. We need Mr. Sangong's help."

"You can tell me," I say more gently. "Mr. Sangong's a kind man. I'm sure he'll be prepared to help."

The girl's hands start to shake, and she opens her bag. Reaching in, she pulls out something wrapped in soft white cloth. I can see light pulsing faintly through the muslin.

Ever so gently, she unwraps the bundle. Inside is an oblong sphere, like a large egg, covered with etching so delicate and intricate it would make Fabergé weep. The sphere is pale blue, and it pulses softly, like the rhythm of a heartbeat. My eyes widen with shock.

I've heard of these before, but never thought I would see one in person—a pari-pari egg.

I look at the couple in amazement. No wonder I couldn't figure out what they were. There are very few pari-pari left, and they're extremely secretive. I know very little about them other than they're like a kind of Asian forest fae who favour slightly cooler climates rather than the humid, tropical countries like Indonesia or southern Thailand.

By all accounts, their difficulties in breeding mean that they're obsessively careful about keeping their eggs and their young out of sight. What on earth could have pushed those two to bring their egg here tonight?

"You should wrap it back up," I tell the girl. I reach beyond my discretion walls to make sure no one is watching or listening. My magic may feed off Mr. Sangong's, but there are still plenty who would be far more powerful than I am.

"We don't have money," the beau says stiffly, "but we can do an agreement as payment to get our egg out of Panong and to London—we have relatives there."

Even the Mayak have a need for money, so some trades are done for cash, but an agreement is like a magical IOU, and being owed a favour by a powerful creature can be extremely valuable.

"We brought an extractor," the girl says quickly. She opens her handbag again, this time pulling out what looks like a needleless, snub-nosed syringe made of magical glass.

I raise both eyebrows. She and her beau looked so hapless on arriving, but they've thought this through, and they have some serious determination. For a pari-pari to give up an egg is as shockingly disturbing as a Mundane mother tossing her baby in the bin. It's just inconceivable.

The girl relaxes her glamour, and her eyes turn from dark to a swirling gold-dusted green that's very similar to the aurora borealis. Her skin is violet and covered with delicate golden patterns. Her clothing has an odd, almost lichen-like texture to it, leaving her arms and most of her legs bare. Her wings have that delicate segmentation as is found in dragonflies, but some of the sections are a deep, translucent green, making her wings look like the most gossamer-fine stained-glass windows. Now that her glamour is lowered, a gentleness rolls off her, something that makes me think of the peacefulness of trees.

She applies the extractor to her tear duct, and a golden tear is sucked into the glass. Her tear looks more like smoke than water, and it moves and coils within the extractor. By the time the girl passes the extractor to her boyfriend, she looks like an ordinary girl again.

The beau's eyes are a deep, shadowy purple, and his skin glows silver. His teeth are black, all of them sharpened to points. His wings are leathery, a bit like a bat's. The sense I get from him is of the cool quiet found in the depths of a cave. His tear is purple streaked with silver. It coils around the golden tear, as if recognising it.

"And you're really sure you want to send your egg to London?" I ask them.

There isn't much old forest left in England. It would be a difficult place for a pari-pari to exist.

The beau nods jerkily and hands me the extractor a little forcefully, so much so that I nearly drop it. The extractor gives me, and only me, the ability to call on the favour whenever I want, but because I'm Mr. Sangong's protégée, I can pass the favour onto him. Which of course I will do the moment he's back in the shop.

The girl's so anxious, she's chewing the inside of her cheeks, her mouth working compulsively. She digs through her handbag again and pulls out a piece of folded paper. "The address of our relatives in London." She thrusts it at me.

"H-how long until you can do it?" the beau asks.

"It'll take a bit of time." I take the paper. I'm starting to feel real sorry for them, now—and a little worried too. What could be so bad that they'd be willing to go this far? Their egg would hatch without them present. I don't actually know what happens when a pari-pari egg hatches, nor do I know anyone who's ever witnessed a hatching. But I do know it's something important and highly secret.

"Can you tell me what's going on?" I ask. "Whatever it is, maybe Mr. Sangong can help."

The girl shakes her head. "Please just... please get our egg to safety." She hands me the cloth-wrapped bundle.

The boy looks so pale he's almost green. He's gripping her shoulder, his hand white-knuckled. The girl squares her shoulder and looks me in the eye, steeling her features.

"What about your names?" I ask.

"You don't need them," the girl replies. "The extractor ensures that you'll be able to call on us."

That kind of secrecy is more in keeping with normal pari-pari behaviour, but I'm not sure how comfortable I feel about not having any frame of reference as to who they are. Still, I suppose if there's anything important enough, I can use the extractor to summon them, as the girl said. And Mr. Sangong will know what to do.

"Please," the girl says. "All we want is for our egg to be safe."

"I'll make sure it is."

"Thank you," she whispers.

Then she takes her beau by the hand, and they both walk out.

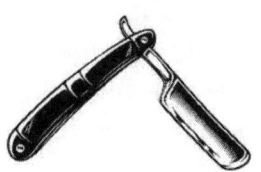

5

I stay put with the egg for a time, a little dumbstruck by the whole encounter and exhilarated too. Normally Mr. Sangong would have handled all that, and I'd have seen none of it. I feel a quick stab of guilt. It might have been better for the couple if they'd been able to see him rather than make do with me.

I take a breath. Ari and the werecat finished their drinks earlier and have already left, so I'm alone with Tim. I'm about to step beyond my privacy walls when a cold shiver of warning ripples down my spine. I freeze. I have absolutely no idea what caused it, but I *always* listen to my intuition.

Safety. The girl asked me to get her egg to safety. That means things aren't safe right now. What if someone's watching the shop, someone who can get past Mr. Sangong's security as well as my privacy walls? Well, if they can get past Mr. Sangong's security, my walls will be as effective as a spider's web against a hurricane. But all the same, I just don't feel comfortable stepping out into the open right now. Better to take precautions.

"Tim," I call in a low voice. "I need you here."

Tim, however, doesn't budge from his chair. He has both eyes closed, but I know he's not sleeping.

"Tim," I hiss.

He can hear me, but the little bugger is obviously paying me back for chucking him out of the office earlier.

"*Tim!*"

He finally cracks and eyelid and gives me a look full of feline contempt. "Cats don't answer to inferiors."

I'm not going to lie, I could strangle him. I swallow my pride and my annoyance. "Oh, wise master, this unworthy one humbly begs you to grant her your assistance with this greatly important task."

Tim yawns, displaying a shockingly pink tongue. He blinks at me slowly once. Then finally, he begins the lengthy process of stretching. He's making it last much longer than he needs, but I know better than to rush him or snap at him. That would make him go back to his nap, just to piss me off.

After what seems like an eternity, he saunters over to me.

"Jesus, what took you so long?" I whisper harshly at him. I barrel on before he can answer. "The couple who left before were two pari-pari, and they left me their egg."

"What? Are they barmy or what? Why would they do that?"

"Look we can talk about it later. For now, I'm worried that in the open, it's vulnerable. The pari-pari were spooked, Tim. Real spooked. If there's someone out there watching the shop..."

"Oh yeah. You can't move your privacy walls with you, can you?" Tim asks smugly.

"You know I can't."

"What must it be like to be so bloody useless?"

"Seriously not the time, Tim. She asked me to send her egg to safety. That means things aren't safe right now—we can't take chances."

"Fine, fine," Tim grumbles. He's a pain in the ass, but he's a good sort, deep down. *Deep,* deep down.

I check to make sure the egg's properly wrapped up. It's not as fragile as a chicken's egg, so dropping it on the floor shouldn't smash it—at least I don't think so. I hope not. Suddenly I really wish Mr. Sangong was here to deal with this. I couldn't live with myself if I managed to break the pari-pari's egg.

Once I've made sure the egg is secure, I hand the little parcel over to Tim, who delicately takes the top of the cloth wrapping between his teeth. His hackles raise up, and a shiver runs down his spine.

My privacy walls suddenly shrink, so they're only covering him. Now that I'm outside of them, I can't really make Tim out anymore. I know he's here, so I still have an awareness of him, but if somebody new came into the shop, they wouldn't notice him. For me, it's almost like the lighting and the angle I'm standing at are conspiring to make it really difficult to get a clear visual of him. And I can't see what he's carrying.

He trots to the office. Keeping a careful sense out for anyone arriving, I follow him and close the door behind us, triggering the barbershop's most powerful privacy spell.

Tim hops up onto the desk and gently puts down the egg. "So, what d'you plan to do with it?" He gives me a sly look. "I know a bloke in London who can find buyers for anything..."

I glare at him. "Are you completely heartless?"

"Jeez, relax. I was only joking."

"Hilarious. My sides are splitting. Can you be serious for a while so we can deal with this important situation? Has it occurred to you that if the pari-pari are that scared, it could be something serious that will affect us all?"

Tim begins to wash his face. This time he isn't flipping me the bird. Instead he's hiding the fact that he feels a bit sheepish. Cats *never* admit to being wrong.

"I'm going to send Mr. Sangong a message," I tell him. "This is way beyond my pay grade."

Tim must *definitely* be feeling sheepish since he doesn't take the opportunity to remind me yet again of my inferior status. He likes to do that a lot.

I pull out my phone and quickly type a text. Calling Mr. Sangong is pointless—if he doesn't want to be disturbed, no ring tone in the world will be able to get through to him. And for some reason, he never returns calls. Sending him messages is also tricky because, while he's perfectly capable of operating technology, he often forgets that his phone exists.

I guess that's the problem with being hundreds or maybe even thousands of years old—the invention of the mobile phone to him is like a tiny footnote at the end of a huge encyclopaedia. He's only just getting used to the existence of computers.

The message sent, I look back at the egg. I have no idea what to do with it. Does it need to be warmed or incubated like a chicken's egg? Is it more like a reptile egg, and it can stay on its own? Or is it something entirely different? I really wish I'd taken the time to ask the pari-pari couple more about how to handle it. But the whole thing went so fast it didn't occur to me back then.

And it's hardly as if I can look up what to do on Wikipedia. I glance at my phone, hoping today is a day Mr. Sangong remembers to check his messages.

I unwrap the egg and hold it in my hands briefly. It's warm but solid and dry. Maybe the blanket is what keeps it warm rather than needing to be incubated like a chicken's egg. It's not as if pari-pari have bodies designed for incubation, after all.

I wrap it back up. "Do you think the egg will be safe here until I hear back from Mr. Sangong?"

"Maybe put it in the safe," Tim suggests.

"Good idea."

The safe has magic to it, and I'm one of the people it's keyed to. I place my palm against what looks like a smooth expanse of wall covered in dark teal wallpaper, and after a shimmer, a safe door appears. It clicks open. I decide to put the extractor in with the egg. Maybe the pari-pari inside the egg is already able to sense, so it would recognise its parents' signatures, which would be comforting.

I've just finishing locking the safe, when I sense a new customer about to enter the shop. "I better go."

"I'll stay here," Tim replies.

———

I spend the rest of the night tense, straining to sense anything out of the ordinary and suspiciously checking out every client who walks through the door. But nothing goes wrong, and more annoyingly, Mr. Sangong doesn't reply.

I'm cleaning up for the night, the sun is about to rise, and I'm seriously considering sleeping in the office to keep an eye on the egg, when my phone finally beeps with a message.

Just leave the egg with Tim, and it will be fine. Go talk to Sarroch about it.

And that's it. Nothing more.

I bite my lip, re-reading the message several times. When Mr. Sangong turned down my offer of help earlier tonight, I assumed he was chastising me, but what if he wasn't? Maybe this is his attempt at delegation.

I have to admit I wasn't expecting him to task me with something so important. I was thinking more along the lines of carrying messages or whatever the magical equivalent of making coffee at a meeting is.

On top of which, I'm not sure that leaving a cat in charge of an egg is a smart idea. And then there's the fact that I don't even know who or what Sarroch is.

I reply, asking about Sarroch.

You're smart enough to figure that out, Apiya.

All right, then, that's clear enough. Mr. Sangong is delegating, and I'm finally being brought deeper into the Mayak world, like I've always wanted. I feel a spike of excitement and nerves.

A bit of googling reveals that Sarroch Industries is a large shipping company and that it's named after its CEO and founder. I guess that's where I'm going later today, after I've caught up on sleep.

I pop back into the office to check on Tim. He's back in the same position as I found him—sleeping on the desk. I swear, that cat does nothing other than sleep on the desk or on the chair next to the bar. He can leave if he wants, roam outside and hang out with other cats, but he rarely does.

"Mr. Sangong says to leave the egg with you, that it'll be safe."

He doesn't lift his head from where it's resting on his paws. "Safe as houses."

"Okay, good to know. I've got to get some information from Sarroch."

"Good luck."

"Do you know him. Her?"

Tim opens an eye, looks at me with contempt, and closes it. I'm not sure why that deserved contempt, but that's cats for you.

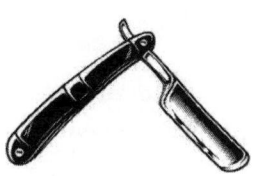

6

I lock up the barbershop and head home. Working nights can take its toll if you're not careful, so I'm religious about my sleep.

I'm halfway back when my phone rings. It's my mother. I should clarify at this point that my parents are British, white, and that they adopted me when I was a baby. They brought me back to England when I was five.

Now, I know what you're thinking. Tattoos, pink hair, biker boots, *and* adopted? You're probably expecting family angst.

You really shouldn't stereotype.

I take the call. "Ahoy, mothership!" I say in English. Although my parents are fluent in Panongian, the habit of talking to them in English is too strongly engrained and I always switch when talking to them.

"Darling, prepare yourself. I fear we have lost your father," Mum says in a dramatic voice.

"Oh, Mama, no! Tell me it isn't true!" I reply, doing my best southern belle accent. Which admittedly isn't great, but I do love doing it.

"It is, darling. He was last seen diving into an illumi-
nated eleventh-century manuscript, and—"

"I'm right here, and I can hear you," Dad calls out in the
background.

"I fear we may never see him again," Mum continues.
"I'm trying to come to terms with being a widow at *such* a
young age. I may have to drown my sorrows with a young,
handsome man—"

There's a brief scuffle underpinned by laughter, then my
dad is on the phone. "It's incredible what your mother
mistakes for humour."

"Oh, happy days, Papa!" I exclaim, still doing my
southern belle. "The manuscript didn't claim you as we'd
feared. I don't have to be an orphan quite yet. To think you
might have left me alone in the world, destitute, begging in
the streets like Oliver Twist while Mum wears leopard print
and cavorts with twenty-year-old men—"

"It also amazes me that even though you're adopted,
you've managed to inherit your mother's sense of humour."

"What?" I cry. "I'm *adopted*? And there I thought I was
the fruit of your loins."

I can practically hear my father roll his eyes as he hands
the phone back to my mother. "She's your daughter."

"Actually, Dad," I call. "I do have a genuine question for
you."

"A question for you," my mother echoes.

He comes back on the phone. "Another joke? I'm forced
to use the term loosely, obviously."

"No, serious this time. What do you know about the
pari-pari?"

"Pari-pari... they're forest creatures." Dad's tone
changes immediately to that mixture of intensity and
excitement anytime the subject of mythological creatures

comes up. Of course they're not mythological but very real. "Forest spirit isn't quite right," he continues, "although I do believe they have a very close symbiotic relationship with trees—or perhaps with tree spirits. Sometimes they're confused with the orang bunian, but they're quite different. The orang bunian make a whistling—"

"Dad? The pari-pari?" I know better than to let him go off on a tangent or I'll never get the info I want.

"Oh yes, right. The accounts I've read of them—and there aren't that many, actually—seem to indicate they're benevolent creatures. Very shy, very secretive. Probably why there isn't much about them. If they truly exist..." My dad pauses. He still does that sometimes, overwhelmed by the thought that the mythical creatures he's been reading about all these years are real and that most of them need barbering.

"They're probably struggling," my mother says. "If they live in symbiosis with trees, deforestation isn't going to be helping them."

Could that be why the couple gave me their egg? Panong has been seeing a lot of construction of late. But in that case, surely they'd be leaving *with* their egg, and they certainly wouldn't want to go to England of all places.

"Dad, what do you know about their eggs?"

"Their eggs? I'll have to do some digging." The latter is said with relish.

My dad is a scholar, a professor of ancient religions and mythology. He's the king of esoteric knowledge and dead languages. Need ancient oracle bones engraved with Archaic Chinese translated and put into context? He's your man. Need someone to help you navigate your way through a Parisian airport? He's as lost as a dyslexic man who's been handed an encyclopaedia in a foreign language. Without an index.

Honestly, if it weren't for my mother—who's an environmental biologist—I really have no idea how he would have survived this long. The only thing he can cook is boiled eggs. Sometimes he manages to screw up even that—oh yes, it is possible, and in ways you couldn't imagine—and the first time we gave him a smartphone, he looked at it like a chicken would look at a can opener. Things haven't improved much since then, either, and it's been a couple of years. He should exchange notes with Mr. Sangong on the variety of ways to *not* use a mobile phone.

But he's also fluent in Panongian, knows all about their more obscure and ancient myths, and when my magical abilities began to manifest with puberty, he took it in his stride. In fact, it was his idea that I should come and study at the Panong university so I'd have the opportunity to connect with others like me and become more deeply acquainted with my heritage.

I'm also pretty sure that he's my best shot at finding out anything of use about pari-pari eggs.

"Why the sudden interest in the pari-pari?" my mother asked.

In other circumstances, I would have told them. But the look in the pari-pari girl's eyes and her plea that I send her egg to safety hold me back.

"Just because a couple walked into the shop today," I reply. "And I've never seen any before." Anyone watching would have known that, and I make it sound casual, like my question is due to nothing more than curiosity.

"Hmmm." My mother has an uncanny ability to detect the slightest untruth—at least from me. She doesn't press the point, though.

"I'll go see what I can find on them right now, honey," my father says.

"Darling, it's nearly eleven p.m.," my mother says. "We're going to sleep, and you can look into all this come morning."

"It's fine. I won't be long. I'll just—"

"You'll just get sucked into one of your rabbit holes, then you won't sleep at all tonight, which isn't good for you," my mother says firmly. "Apiya's research can wait until tomorrow."

My dad grouses for good measure, but of course he'll do as my mother says. They sign off.

Hopefully Dad will get me something useful—even once I've arranged the transport for the egg, I have no real idea how to pack it or what it would need for the journey. What happens if it hatches midway? Can it hatch midway?

I feel a brief flare of irritation. If I weren't so far on the fringes of the Mayak, and if Mr. Sangong hadn't kept me so sheltered, I would have a bit more knowledge about these things.

I really want to help the pari-pari, but right now, I'm feeling about as qualified for the job as an octopus trying to thread a needle.

7

I don't normally like to stereotype, but in this instance, the cliché is true. I live with the dumbest blonde ever. I truly mean it.

I unlock the front door and step in to be greeted by thirty kilos of manically excited, wiggling golden fur. Hunter, my golden retriever, always goes into paroxysms of joy any time I step through the door—and it doesn't matter whether I've been gone for five minutes or five hours. I have to admit I absolutely love him for it.

I go through the usual ritual of asking him "who's a good boy? Who's a very good boy? Who's the bestest boy in the world?" and petting him enthusiastically, until he's in danger of overdosing on excitement. Then I throw him a treat. He fails to catch it, as usual.

Hunter is optimistically named, if you assume he's named for the ability to hunt. Once the treat falls to the floor, he looks around for it, fails to find it, despite it being less than a metre away, then looks back at me, eagerly anticipating the next one.

I actually named my dog after Hunter S. Thompson, and

clearly, I subconsciously named him for when the gonzo journalist was roaring drunk and useless.

"Go on, Hunter! Find your treat!" I call as I take off my boots and put them on the shoe rack.

He glances around him again, again fails to spot the treat, then looks up at me enthusiastically, tongue lolling in a smile. Such a handsome boy.

I point out the treat for him, getting his muzzle to follow my finger. Once he spots the treat, he pounces on it, full of joyful surprise. I love my dog—I *adore* my dog. But he's so dumb he verges on untrainable. I don't say this lightly, either. When I failed to get any results by myself, I took him to a fancy dog trainer with all the qualifications and certificates. I had to eat instant noodles for months and borrow money to pay for the private sessions. After several months, the trainer gave up, refunded most of my money, and admitted he'd never encountered a dog so impervious to training.

But Hunter's got the best temperament. He's a darling. He's handsome—so what if he never comes when I call or will never understand the command "wait"? I love him to bits anyway. Not like his last family.

Hunter was abandoned by an American expat family who left Panong to return home and obviously didn't want to go through the hassle and expense of flying him back with them. I found him tied to a post, hungry, severely dehydrated, and heartbroken. He hasn't left my side since.

A little sleuthing helped me identify the family who had abandoned him. It became clear very quickly that official channels would do nothing and that the family would get away with no repercussions for what they did to Hunter. Lucky for me, the Touched network is wide. I called every contact and favour I had, and after an enormous amount of effort, I got the family cursed so no dog would be willing to approach them ever again.

I also had someone shove dog poo through their letterbox. Childish, but satisfying. Even more satisfying was that a police dog went mental at their car, barking at them because of the curse, and when the police officer had the dog sniff the car properly, it discovered a bag of cocaine in the father's coat.

Poetic justice for another dog to give Hunter the retribution he deserved. Don't you think?

Hunter's not my only rescue, though. I'm a sucker for any creature that's been abandoned or mistreated. Feel free to pull out your pop-psychology manuals and link that to the fact that I'm adopted. I don't mind. Plus, I like having animals around.

The rest of them mostly live outside in a little walled courtyard that extends from the kitchen. There's a dog flap so Hunter can pop in and out when I'm not around.

"Fergie," I scold as I open the door and step outside. "What the hell are you doing?"

Ferguson—Fergie to his close friends—has somehow managed to wedge himself between the trellis and the brick courtyard wall, but he's not at ground level. Oh no. That would be far too tame for Fergie. He's about a foot off the floor, having somehow managed to climb up the trellis a little before getting stuck. His shell is well wedged, so his little stubby legs waggle uselessly.

I disengage him gently.

Fergie is a rescue from a fellow Touched who had to make an extremely rushed departure from Panong. I never found out why she had to flee—it's best not to meddle in others' magical business—but I happily took Fergie in for her. I don't know if a tortoise can be Touched, but I've never heard of tortoises with climbing abilities before, so there has to be a little something magical about him.

I have a variety of hutches and shelters for the rest of my menagerie. Birds who can't fly due to injuries or clipped wings—from previous owners, I would *never* do that—a couple of rabbits, a guinea pig who's also had some contact with the Touched and as a result is able to communicate by squeaking in morse code—he mostly squeaks the word "lettuce"—and even an Asian painted frog who lives in the tiny pond I built for him. He sings for mates at night, poor thing. I need to find him a girl, but that's harder than you might expect because I refuse to take one from the wild.

You'd think my place would get messy with so many animals, but this is the kind of thing my magic is good for. Don't get ahead of yourself—I can't flat-out move things or manipulate things or anything fancy like that. So I can't just click my fingers and make all the dog hair disappear.

Instead it looks more like luck. Hunter's hair mostly falls outside in the courtyard. My animals mostly stay where I want them to—Fergie's the exception—and they all do their business outside. Things mostly stay as clean and tidy as I like them to be. Yes, I'd make an amazing housewife. *That's* how great my magic is.

To be honest, I don't really understand how my magic works, and neither does Mr. Sangong, although he has never admitted as much to me. I'm like Hunter—untrainable. We're birds of a feather, another reason I adore him.

My magic feels more like I'm making *suggestions* and the objects respond. It tends to work best when I know the objects well, and when my suggestions are compatible with the object's true nature. If I'm in a completely new setting, there's very little I can do. But here, on my territory, things just... *cooperate* with me. At least that's the best way I can explain it. I can't make things go against their nature, but I can encourage them to work better or maintain themselves more effectively.

Of course I can only do this with things that don't have a will of their own. Animals I can nudge a teeny tiny bit (not Hunter). Humans and Mayak? Forget about it.

I'm feeling pretty tired, but I still take Hunter out for a long walk. That done, I collapse into a dreamless sleep. I wake up in the afternoon, at which point Hunter gets a second walk, then it's time to get ready to go see what the deal is with this Sarroch person.

8

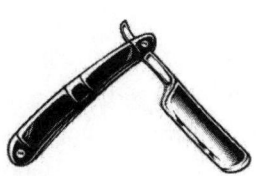

Sarroch Industries' offices are across town, so I put on my black riding leathers and walk out to where my bike is parked. It's a 1960s Triumph Bonneville T120 with a renovated engine, basically like a modern engine hidden behind those beautiful, classic curves. It helps to have a friend whose magic revolves around metal.

The ride across town is pretty satisfying. The road infrastructure in Panong isn't great, and it's certainly not able to deal with the recent influx of new cars on the road.

Panong has mostly managed to stay off everyone's radars until recently. It could have ended up like Hong Kong, attracting colonial attention until it was thoroughly ruined, turned into a busy trading port that makes plenty of money. The British did eventually make their way to Panong, but they only colonised it as an afterthought and did virtually nothing to it. They had Hong Kong and Singapore and all their other territories by then.

Panong's a little island due south of Hong Kong, slap bang between Vietnam and the Philippines. It doesn't have the kind of access to the bigger countries that the British

Empire wanted. Nobody really remembers the British presence here. They came, established an ambassador or two, then they left. I don't think we could even qualify as a footnote to the British Empire. We were a non-event.

Panong didn't have much in the way of valuable resources, and its people were—and still are—so superstitious and full of traditions, westerners find it difficult to do business with us. Back then it would have been even worse.

Tourism passed us by, as well. We're a volcanic island, so our beaches are black sand—an instant tourism turn off (thank god for that). The volcanic hills that occupy most of the centre of the island make it hard to build too.

It's this lack of development that caused the Mayak to flock here in high numbers starting about a century ago.

Panong has developed in recent years, though, and the increase in money means an increase of cars on the road, instead of the usual scooters and small motorbikes. During workdays, the roads are basically one long succession of bottlenecks, cars cramming in to try and fit down little roads that weren't designed for heavy motorised traffic.

On my bike, though, I'm nimble, so I weave through the traffic along with all the other motorbikes and scooters. It's pretty satisfying.

I pull up outside Sarroch Industries, frowning as I remove my helmet. It's one of those new high-rises we've been seeing an increasing number of lately. Panong technically has a financial district, but it's so small and pathetic, very little goes on there, and foreign investment has always remained minimal—at least until recently.

I'm surprised, though, that one of the Mayak would be comfortable in such a building. The Mayak still think of the 1920s as a modern era... hence attitudes like Mr. Sangong's inability to remember that his phone exists. Normally the

Mayak exist in the old, forgotten areas, abandoned buildings, the nooks and crannies where gloom and secrecy still reign.

Evidence of the morning's rainfall remains—beads of water cling to the glass and metal surfaces of the building. On the ground floor, a glass revolving door swings, letting people in and out. Beyond, I can see a black polished counter manned by two women with long, sleek ponytails. In gold letters, behind them, the words Sarroch Industries are spelled out.

I push my way through the revolving door, my helmet tucked under my left arm. Everyone's footsteps echo loudly inside the lobby, the sounds bouncing off the high ceilings and hard, gleaming surfaces.

I make my way over to the reception counter. "I need to see..." I cough, making a sound that could be either Mr. or Mrs. "Sarroch, please." I should have double-checked the gender. I also should have checked the full name again—I can't even remember whether Sarroch is a first name or surname. My first assignment and I'm flubbing it like a teenager in a maths test.

"Do you have an appointment?"

"No, but it's urgent. Please tell him that Mr. Sangong sent me."

"Your name?"

"Apiya Chapman."

The woman looks surprised—that'll be the effect of my last name. We don't have many foreigners in Panong. I'm really not in the mood to have the conversation about why I have an English surname.

Luckily, she either senses that, or receptionists are not supposed to ask visitors questions. "Have a seat please."

My riding leathers squeak against the leather of the

waiting chair as I sit down. I only have to wait ten minutes before one of the women—with a faint expression of surprise—escorts me to the elevator. I'm given a VIP visitor's pass and told to come straight back down once I'm done with my appointment.

The glass elevator zips up the building, taking me to the top floor—of course. Businessmen are so predictable. Everything's a pissing contest to them, so they'll always try to have the highest office, the latest piece of fancy tech, and all that nonsense.

Again, I'm surprised a Mayak would play along with this kind of thing. Status works differently in the magical community, and being so enmeshed in the Mundane world wouldn't be looked upon very favourably. At least that's my understanding, but I could be wrong.

It's not until I reach another reception counter manned by another ponytailed woman that it occurs to me that Sarroch might not be part of the Mayak. Mr. Sangong didn't say so, and few Mayak would take on such a visible position. Keeping out of sight of the Mundanes is the name of the game, after all.

The secretary escorts me to Sarroch's office, her long black ponytail swinging behind her. Her stiletto heels look like they could be used to gouge someone's eye out, and her pencil skirt forces her to take lots of ridiculously tiny steps.

She opens a tall door that makes a slight suction noise and gestures me inside. As I step through, the door closes behind me with a slight click and a sense of a seal having been formed.

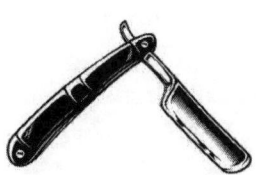

9

F loor-to-ceiling windows give—I'm a little chagrined to have to admit—quite an impressive view over the Luyang Temple, the oldest one in Panong. Its jade tiles gleam from the leftover rainwater.

Directly in front of me is a desk with two chairs facing it and a man sitting behind it, slightly bent over as he writes something with a Montblanc pen.

Although there are papers and other items on the desk, everything is meticulously organised, every last sheet of paper either neatly piled on top of others or properly lined up so as to be parallel with the edges of the desk.

A man after my own heart.

I try to sense him discreetly, but I get an odd signature, nothing I recognise. Another creature I haven't encountered before?

Sarroch looks far younger than I'd have expected, late thirties at the most. Of course, if he's a powerful Mayak, he's likely hundreds of years older than that and just chose a young-looking glamour.

He hasn't even looked up at my arrival, which annoys

me. I wasn't expecting a welcome parade, but at least a nod of acknowledgement would be nice. I consider informing him of that fact, but displaying any impatience would show me to have the heart of a child, which would cause me, and Mr. Sangong as my mentor, to lose face.

A *really* bad way to start the meeting. I don't want Mr. Sangong to hear that I botched the very first assignment he gave me, so I wait.

Patiently. The Mayak are also sometimes referred to as the Patient Ones. Another reason why I'm not a Mayak...

And I'm still waiting.

I take a deep breath (Sarroch still hasn't looked up) and distract myself by giving him the once over, see if I can glean any clues about him from his glamour.

The appearance he chose isn't just young-looking, it's good-looking too. Cheekbones that could cut glass and a sensuous mouth. I can't see his eyes, though, because of the angle at which he's bending his head. The eyes make all the difference—ever seen a really handsome guy with sunglasses on only to be disappointed when the sunglasses come off?

Yeah. I'm reserving final judgement.

Normally young and good-looking glamours mean a Mayak who's still young enough to be vain. Or maybe he's a male pontianak—nasty, bloodthirsty spirits who take on beautiful appearances and feed on humans to maintain their looks. I've only ever seen one in the barbershop, a female, and she terrified me. Mr. Sangong took care of her.

Actually, now that I think of it, I'm not sure there's such a thing as a male pontianak. I'll have to ask Dad. And if Sarroch is a pontianak, I'd be able to pick up something faintly familiar since I've already encountered that kind before. But the faint signature I can pick up is utterly foreign. Unless pontianaks are able to mask their signatures, like Mr. Sangong.

I sigh. Struggling to keep up with the convoluted aspect of Mayak signatures makes me feel far more inadequate than anything the Mayak say or do.

Sarroch finally looks up. His eyes are dark, liquid brown, and serious—the eyes of a mourner. He passes a hand through his hair, pushing the inky strands back from his forehead. Okay, yeah, he's handsome. Annoyingly so.

"You said Sangong sent you?" He gestures at the chairs in front of his desk. "Please sit..."

I take a seat.

"I hadn't realised Sangong had taken on another apprentice. I guess he's making you man his barbershop and run his errands." Sarroch shakes his head. "That barbershop of his—what a waste of time. But better he give that kind of work to a Touched, I suppose."

I bristle. I love the barbershop, and I most definitely don't think of it as a waste of time. "I'm Apiya," I say curtly.

Sarroch raises an eyebrow but doesn't comment on my tone. Instead he says, "How can I help?"

"Mr. Sangong sent me because..." I don't get the cold shiver of warning, but all the same, I don't feel comfortable talking about the egg to this man I know nothing about. If he'd been recommended by anyone other than Mr. Sangong, I wouldn't have.

"Yes?"

I'm really not supposed to question a higher-ranking Mayak, but at the same time, that pari-pari couple trusted me with their most prized possession—their egg. I know Mr. Sangong wouldn't have sent me here if Sarroch couldn't be trusted, but all the same. I don't feel comfortable taking risks with the pari-pari's egg.

"What's your relationship with Mr. Sangong?" I ask.

"Shouldn't you be asking your master that?"

I shrug. "He's not here, but you are. And the matter at hand is incredibly sensitive, so I need to have a sense of who I'm dealing with before I speak of it."

"If you didn't think I was trustworthy, why come here?"

"Because Mr. Sangong told me you'd be able to help. Can you?"

"I don't know. I don't know what you need help with."

As the saying goes, ask stupid questions, get stupid answers. I try another tack. "If I tell you what we're dealing with, will you help without trying to take advantage of the situation for your own gain?" Better wording.

Sarroch considers me for a moment. "Sure."

I lick my lips, feeling a twinge of nerves. If I don't trust Sarroch, I insult Mr. Sangong's judgement, and probably Sarroch too. I also have no other avenues to turn to in order to deal with the egg. "I was approached by a pari-pari couple last night."

Sarroch's eyebrows rise. "Were you, now?"

I nod. "Something's got them scared. Real scared. They... they gave me something of theirs to look after. Something precious that I need to send away from Panong. Mr. Sangong thought you'd be able to help with that."

"They gave you something precious..." His eyes widen. "They gave you their egg?"

I jump to my feet, stumbling back. "You do not have permission to take from my thoughts," I snarl.

If he managed that without me feeling anything, he's real good. Dangerously good. I put a mental wall up like Mr. Sangong showed me, but I very much doubt it will be enough if Sarroch wants to get past it. I suddenly feel incredibly vulnerable.

He waves his hand dismissively. "I didn't take from your thoughts. I didn't need to since I'm able to think for myself. Eggs are the only thing pari-pari have that is precious to them. Precious enough that you'd be this jumpy telling me about it." He leans towards me, eyes intent. "You have it? You have the egg?"

I nod. Not quite the truth, not quite a lie, since it's at the barbershop. He sits back in his chair, face unreadable.

"We need to speak of this somewhere a little more... private. My office isn't appropriate. Come and find me at the Crane. And bring the egg."

Now it's my turn to raise an eyebrow. "The Crane is *private*?"

"It is for me when I need to have meetings there. I have a private room." Sarroch must be seriously important if he can commandeer a private room at the Crane. "Come at one a.m."

"I'm not a member," I say dryly.

The Crane is a club that only caters to the Mayak. The *true* Mayak, as some like to call themselves—meaning that the Touched aren't allowed to hold membership and generally aren't welcome.

"I'll make sure your signature is at the door." If getting me into a private room at the Crane is that easy for Sarroch, he must have some serious clout among the Mayak. The more powerful members don't like having Touched around, so Sarroch would have to be able to face up to them.

I wonder again what he might be, but before I can think on it more, he leans forward, hand out, eyes locked onto mine.

I don't like giving someone I don't know my signature—it's too oddly intimate. But I know there's no other option. Given glamours and shapeshifting abilities, the Mayak put no stock in appearances. Same with names—the older creatures have had too many names to keep track of. Mundane names are changed with the same ease as clothes. And True Names, well that would be like giving someone access to the very depths of your soul—far too dangerous for something as simple as entering a club.

I grudgingly put my hand in Sarroch's. His grip is firm and warm, and his eyes stay locked onto mine. I know this is part of the process, but all the same, it makes me shiver. I feel like prey that just got caught in a predator's snare.

I do my best to relax and ignore the feeling, letting him sense my magic. It's as weird and awkward as letting someone you don't know get right up close and give you a good sniff. Over time, once you get to know someone, you eventually pick up their signature without needing to do this. But it takes a lot of time.

Sarroch's eyes bore into mine as he memorises my signature. They're like twin black pools—I could have sworn his eyes were brown before. I feel an odd sensation of falling, and I see something gold flicker deep within his irises... and then I yank my hand away and break the moment.

I've never experienced that before when giving someone my signature. But then again, I've never given my signature to someone truly powerful. Mr. Sangong and my clients got my signature gradually, as they got to know me.

Could it be that I experienced a reaction to being in contact with larger amounts of magic than I'm used to?

Sarroch nods at me. "See you tonight."

I hesitate, half tempted to ask about what I felt, then I decide I'll ask Mr. Sangong instead. I don't know about Sarroch, and if he was trying to pull something on me, asking him about it won't help.

I leave the office, making my way back outside. It's only

once I take a breath of damp air that it hits me. I'm going to the Crane tonight. I feel a small shiver of excitement as I leave. I've always wanted to see what it's like at the Crane.

I take a final glance at Sarroch Industries' building as I walk away, wondering who Sarroch truly is, and more importantly *what* he is.

10

After leaving Sarroch, I text Mr. Sangong to inform him of my invitation to the Crane. Unsurprisingly, I get no reply. Then I take Hunter out for a long run up in the hills and let him stretch his legs off-leash. He chases after a few red-bellied squirrels, but of course fails to get anywhere near them, and I'm pretty sure the squirrels are taunting him. He has a good time, though.

And then, of course, he finds some kind of poo and rolls in it, running back to me with a big doggie grin, reeking worse than a week-old corpse.

When we get home, it takes me a while to clean him off. He's done a thorough job—the poo is properly ingrained in his fur. Fun, fun, fun—especially when he tries to enthusiastically lick me while I'm knuckle-deep in his fur, scrubbing him with soap.

Once that's finally done, I head over to the gym for a Muay Thai sparring session. I'm as religious about keeping fit as I am about my sleep. Given how weak my magic is, I need to make the best of what I have, and sometimes a punch to the nose or a well-aimed kick to the gut can be enough to dissuade someone from causing me trouble. That works best with the shifters who, generally speaking, tend to be more aggressive and therefore respect shows of strength.

The sparring done, I grab Hunter (I've already forgiven him for rolling in poo since he's just too damn handsome for me to stay annoyed with him), and we go to Chai's studio.

Chai has got an amazing loft space in an old warehouse, complete with cast iron columns and wooden beams. Yep, Chai comes from money. And this isn't his apartment, either, just the studio where he works on his sculptures.

I use the heavy cast iron knocker, shaped like an octopus tentacle, curving out of the door. "It's me."

"Come in, petal!" Chai calls out in English.

Chai is full Panongian, but his family sent him to boarding school in England for a few years, where he picked up an accent to rival Stephen Fry's. But whereas I get annoyed with questions about where I'm from, Chai loves anything that makes him stand out as different, so he's been watching British TV shows over the years to practice his accent. Plus it helps with his English-speaking clients, so he always insists that we speak in English to get some extra practice in, and he likes to ham it up any opportunity he gets.

I get a firm grip on Hunter's leash and open the door.

The loft is flooded with light. Enormous floor-to-high-ceiling windows divided into small panes give a view of the sea. Although this is supposed to be a working sculptor's studio, it's pristine. Chai's sculptures are dotted throughout the space, artfully arranged in case a client wants to drop in and see his work.

At the back, he has a work area set up, but that hasn't been touched for as long as I've known him. He moves things around every so often to make it look like it gets used.

Given Chai's abilities with metal, he just shapes it all by hand, and it takes him minutes to accomplish what a Mundane would need days to do. But of course, he can't let the Mundanes know that. His ability with metal does mean he's the most prolific sculptor of his time, and he's become mildly famous for it.

That wasn't always the case. In his early days, he worked as a mechanic to make ends meet, since his family didn't approve of his choice to pursue a career as a sculptor, and they temporarily cut him off. That's how Chai was able to sort out my motorbike.

When he talks about his days as a mechanic, he likes to make out like it was something from a bad eighties movie, all tight trousers and leather tool belts, but I know he took the work seriously—he's actually a good mechanic. His family eventually caved and restored his access to the family money, but these days, he doesn't need it anyway. He's minted in his own right.

He used to do a lot of abstract and unusual shapes, but now, he's really into depicting hair—women's hair to be precise. The nearest statue to me is a woman standing as if braced against the wind. Her hair streams behind her, whipped into a frenzy. The woman herself is average, but her hair is exquisite. I've told Chai my thoughts about the hair and keep my opinions about the rest of the sculpture to myself.

"Api!" Chai beams as he comes towards me, his movements fluid. He looks like he's in his early thirties, willowy and very handsome. He could easily be a model. His eyes always gleam mischievously, as if he's in the middle of doing something bad—which, to be fair, he often is. Great fun to be around. I have no idea of his true age, though. Some of the more powerful Touched age more slowly than

Mundanes. Anytime I ask Chai for his age, he gives me a sly look and tells me that he has the ass of a twenty-one-year-old, and that's all I need to know.

But sometimes he slips up and talks about his days at boarding school, and it was definitely before I was born.

Hunter goes into paroxysms of joy at the sight of him, and it takes a death grip on the leash to stop him from jumping all over Chai.

"One day, you're going to have to figure out how to train him," he says.

"One day, you're going to have to make peace with Hunter showing you love."

"Darling, I love you and Hunter both. I *adore* you. I would take a *bullet* for the two of you. But I won't get covered in dog slobber for you."

Chai opens a cupboard and grabs the special toys he buys Hunter to distract him. It's very effective. Once Hunter is calm and enjoying his new toy, we kiss each other on both cheeks the way the French and the fashionistas do. It's not my kind of thing, but Chai insists on it.

"Wearing your artist's clothes today I see?" I gesture at his head-to-toe black clothing.

"I had a client come by earlier. You know what they're like, sweetie—how are they to know I'm an artist if I don't wear a black cashmere turtleneck accessorised with appropriate levels of existential angst? In fact, your arrival is *divinely* timed—I was boring myself silly over my essay."

I roll my eyes. "Why do you still bother with these explanations of your sculptures if they bore you?"

"*Darling*, it's the expected thing. Given that most modern art looks like a *five*-year-old could have done it, a pompous explanation of what it represents is a must, so people feel like they've spent their money wisely. These days, they *all* expect some tortured explanation of how the wave of the statue's hair represents the freedom of the post-feminist era, that kind of thing. Dreadfully tedious, my sweet, although I've found a shortcut. Feminism is so hot right now that so as long as I mention it, people buy. Unless the piece is geometrical, then I talk about the rigidity of the patriarchy, and if it's a heavy piece, I talk about the *oppression* of the patriarchy."

"People really buy that?"

"The Chinese billionaires don't care about feminism, but I'm trying to expand into Europe. And the London bankers are falling over themselves to appear modern enough to impress their twenty-two-year-old philosophy student mistresses. But *là*, sweet pea, I'm boring you with my work, and I haven't even offered you a drink. Gin martini?"

"Isn't it a bit early for that?"

"Nonsense. On top of wearing a turtleneck, it's important for an artist to drink at inappropriate hours." He heads over to the bar, followed by Hunter with his new toy in his mouth. Now that there's no chance of being covered in slobber, Chai strokes his head and gives him a proper hello. He wasn't lying when he said he adored Hunter. He just can't stand dog slobber. "So to what do I owe the pleasure of this visit?" he asks as he busies himself at his bar.

Chai taught me all about expensive alcohol—it's why I know how to keep the barbershop lounge well-stocked. His own bar is all sleek glass and polished chrome. As with everything else in his studio, it's sharp, spotless, stylish.

"I had an interesting encounter today, and I wanted to get your thoughts."

"Then sit, sit."

I grab one of Chai's stylish and uncomfortable metal-and-leather armchairs. He joins me moments later, handing me a gin martini, which I set aside. It's not even late after-noon—way too early for something so potent.

He rolled up his sleeves before making the martinis, revealing a couple of tattoos on his right arm. They sway gently, like seaweed on the bottom of a seabed, each tattoo a string of symbols.

"You got them topped up?" I ask.

Chai frowns and looks down at his forearm. "Yes, but it's poor. I *still* haven't been able to find a decent tattoo prac-titioner."

As you'll have guessed, the tattoos are imbued with magic, and in Chai's case, they boost his abilities, as they do for all the Touched who get those types of tattoos. I've tried it, but no matter how many tattoos I got, my magic remained weak. The tattoos look cool, so I don't mind too much.

"Now, you were about to tell me all the gossip of your day."

11

I tell him about the pari-pari, and his eyes widen, his impish expression turning serious. "They gave you their egg?"

"Yeah, I know. I felt just as shocked. They were spooked, Chai. Properly spooked. Have you heard anything lately? Anything that could help explain why they'd be so scared?"

He shakes his head. "Nothing. All's been normal, as far as I know."

"Mr. Sangong sent me to Sarroch Industries to ask for assistance in getting the egg shipped to London."

Chai's mischievous expression returns. "Oooh, lucky you. An *intimate*, private meeting with Sarroch. Were your knickers all aflutter?"

I ignore the question. "You know him?"

"Who doesn't?"

"Just me, apparently."

"He's a big-league Mayak. And actually, he was one of the biggest supporters of the rule banning the Touched from using tattoos." His tone is bitter.

"I thought you liked him."

"I find him *hot*, blossom. There's a difference. I dislike him intensely, but that doesn't stop me from admiring the facade."

I can understand Chai's bitterness. The tattoos did wonders for his magic, but they have to be topped up every so often, or they lapse back into regular tattoos. Since the ban, practitioners are much harder to come by, and those willing to risk the wrath of the Mayak by practicing on the black market tend not to be very good.

"Did Sarroch agree to help you?" Chai asks.

"He hasn't given me a real answer. Instead he asked me to meet him at the Crane."

Now Chai looks properly shocked.

"That's why I wanted to get your advice. You've been once before, haven't you?"

"Oh, pudding, I don't think it's a good idea for you to go."

"Is it really that bad?"

"It's really that dangerous. You'd have no protection other than Sarroch's and Mr. Sangong's name. You'd be at the mercy of any Mayak who decided to take offence at a Touched rubbing shoulders with them. And no, the Mayak traditional guesting rules don't apply to the Touched."

"Sarroch is powerful enough to take on anyone with a problem, though, right? At least that's what I assumed since he has a private room there."

"Yes, but if he has to step away?"

"I'll use Mr. Sangong's name."

Chai sighs. "That's a powerful card, but will it be enough?"

The Mayak have strict rules about hunting, in the sense that anything that might attract Mundane attention is forbidden. So that mostly means hunting at night in discreet locations. And it doesn't get more discreet than the Crane.

"Maybe I'll ask Mr. Sangong," I say grudgingly. "See if he can arrange something so I've got protection when I go in there." It feels like an admission of defeat. The first time I get a proper look into the Mayak's world, and I have to ask for hand-holding.

I pull out my phone and fire off another text. Still no reply to the last one.

"To be honest, though, why do you care?" Chai asks. "This egg thing is Mayak business—let the Mayak handle it."

"You didn't see how sad and scared the pari-pari were. I'm not heartless enough to leave them in the lurch."

I don't add that this is also what I've always wanted, getting more involved with the Mayak. That will only get me a lecture. Chai's got a real bee in his bonnet about my magic being weak and me needing protection. A bit like Mr. Sangong, I guess.

Chai's pretty powerful for a Touched. He likes to act like a bit of an airhead, but he's smart, powerful, and a badass in a fight. Which is why he's more immersed in the Mayak world than I am. He can protect himself. And same as Mr. Sangong, he's never agreed to take me anywhere with him. Something that rankles, if I'm completely honest.

"Well, if you go, go with your eyes open," Chai says. "Bring weapons. Whatever's got the pari-pari that scared must be nasty. And guess where the nasty Mayak like to congregate at night?" Chai shakes his head. "Maybe I should come with you."

"Sarroch said nothing about a plus-one, so they probably won't let you in. And making myself look weak or scared won't help."

He sighs. "You're right. I don't like it, but you're right. Well, be careful, and *call* me if you need anything."

We chat for a while longer, then it's time for me to head over to the barbershop for the evening's work. I'll get a few hours in before I have to the leave for the Crane.

"What will you wear at the Crane, by the way?" Chai asks.

I gesture at my clothes—black riding leathers, studded boots, light-grey vest top. Chai arches an eyebrow.

"Is that a problem?" I ask.

"Not for me, darling, but you know I love trash."

I snort with laughter. "What an amazingly backhanded compliment."

"I do my best."

———

I LEAVE HUNTER WITH CHAI AT HIS REQUEST, SINCE HE'S finished working for the day, and for all that he complains about the slobber, he loves hanging out with my dog. He's also still determined to teach Hunter a trick. More power to him.

It does me a favour too. Hunter always gets anxious when I leave, so it makes me feel better to know he's got someone to fuss over him while I'm at work.

I check on the egg and Tim at the barbershop—both are doing fine. I cradle the egg in my hands for a few moments, trying to see if it looks any different from yesterday. It has the same softly, pulsing blue light, the same incredibly delicate etchings, and it still feels just as warm. Points to me for managing to keep it alive for a day.

I send Mr. Sangong yet another message, this time about taking care of the egg and how best to do that. By some miracle, I get a response right away.

So long as you take care of it, the egg will be fine.

I glare at the phone. What kind of answer is that? That's basically the problem. I don't know how to take care of the egg.

"And what about the rest of my other bloody messages?" I mutter in English.

I reply, asking about the Crane and whether he should come with me. No reply. I could play it super safe and not go, wait until I have word from Mr. Sangong, but that will most definitely offend Sarroch, and what are the chances I'll get another opportunity to go?

I decide it will be fine. If it was a bad idea to go, Mr. Sangong would have said something. No answer must mean a tacit go ahead.

I take care of a few clients, then as midnight rolls by, I touch my hand to a stone next to the entrance, infusing it with the message that the barbershop is closed for the night. It will diffuse the message, so anyone approaching it will be able to sense it and won't try coming inside. Then it's time to get going.

The Crane's entrance is at the doorway of an abandoned building on the edge of town, at the foot of one of Panong's oldest volcanic hills that's covered in forest. Nature is busy reclaiming as much of the place as she can, with creepers crawling out the busted windows and a young banyan tree sprouting from the broken roof. At the top of the building is a large, decorative bat, upside down with its wings open and a brass ring coming out of its mouth. Beyond, the night is loud with the sound of insects, the hill stretching up, shrouded in darkness.

There isn't a crack of light from the building, not so much as a whisper of music to give away what the shop truly houses. But then again, the security illusions to keep

Mundanes at bay here will probably make the setup at the barbershop look like child's play.

As I get close to the doors, two door guardians materialise on their surfaces. At first, they're flat, as if two-dimensional or painted, then they step out towards me, growing into fully three-dimensional, living creatures.

The door guardians tower at nearly seven feet tall, made even taller by their red-and-black helmets. Their articulated armour is black and gleams like beetle shells, with huge spikes at their shoulders, and their identical beards and moustaches reach their chests.

"Sarroch is expecting me," I tell them.

One of the guardians extends a hand towards me. His nails are over an inch long, curved like talons, and black. Somehow, I very much doubt door guardians indulge in manicures, so this must be the nails' natural colour.

Doing my best not to shudder, I extend my hand and look the guardian in the eye. In spite of my best efforts, my skin crawls, and a faint shiver rolls down my spine as the guardian leans towards me to sense my signature.

He nods once, and I snatch my hand away. The other guardian waves a hand and the doors slide silently open. I step through.

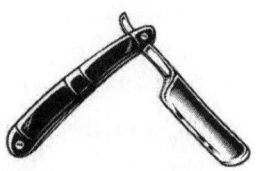

12

I 've heard enough of the Crane to know to expect something still stuck in the 1920s. Which is where a lot of the Mayak seem to prefer existing—there aren't many who have made it into the twenty-first century. Sarroch is one of the few.

As with the barbershop, the space I step into has absolutely no relation to the external space occupied by the building, being several times bigger.

The room is panelled in black glass with golden brass art deco geometric patterns overlaid on it. Smoky shapes move, coiling within the glass. The floor looks like it's lacquered wood—but it can't be. That would be a crazy expense. Then again, who knows with the Mayak? One wall is covered with antique prints of red-crowned cranes, some painted on silk, others on thin wooden board with gold leaf accents. A nod to the name of the club.

Plush black silk and gold booths at the edges of the main room allow couples and small groups to sit and talk. Standing tables are dotted throughout the rest of the space, covered with drinks as people place down their glasses to go talk to someone.

A woman, with hair styled to look wet, curls artfully placed along her forehead and on either side of her face, is talking to a section of the black glass wall, clasping a long cigarette holder in her right hand. Her dress is a twenties drop-waisted collection of glittering fringes. She laughs and touches her left hand to the wall. After only a couple of seconds, she lets out a cry, her smile replaced by anger.

"You take too much!" The hand she withdraws from the glass is bleeding where the pads of her fingers touched the surface.

Smoke coils out of the glass towards her, taking on a vaguely humanoid shape. "More," it says in a breathy voice.

"No," the woman says coldly. She spins away and disappears into the crowd.

The smoke creature looks around, and although it has no eyes, I can feel its gaze settling on me. I make myself scarce.

The room is crowded, but it feels different from a crowd of humans. People here move so sinuously, so gracefully, that it almost looks like they're all dancing to the jazz music being played somewhere further in. An eerily perfect imitation of Louis Jordan's voice croons about whether his baby is still his baby true.

Some people around me have human forms and glamours, some have half glamours, and some are simply wearing their true forms. Those wearing clothes are mostly dressed from the twenties, thirties, and forties. Sequins and fringes and narrow, fitted skirts that skim the contours of their wearers' bodies. I don't see a single pair of jeans in sight. I look all kinds of wrong in my leather motorbike riding gear, clompy boots, and pink hair, but that's nothing new.

I grab the strap of my cross-body satchel partly for reassurance, partly to make sure no one snatches it from me. In it I've stowed my gloves, phone, bike keys, and two of my sharpest razors.

As I move through the crowd, I can sense the magic so powerfully it's like a perfume. The air is charged like before a storm, the amount of magic gathered in such a small space making a faint, almost buzzing sensation against my skin. Like licking a battery, but all over my body.

It's made all the more intense by the knowledge that I'm no match for *anyone* present. If I reach out, I can sense all kinds of useless things—I can sense the floor beneath me, not physically, but using my limited magical senses in the same way I do when I want my animals' hair to fall out in the courtyard rather than indoors.

So yeah, while I'm surrounded by all kinds of powerful supernatural creatures, *I* can help make sure that things like spilt drinks don't stain the lacquer on the floor too badly. Although, since I don't know the floor well enough yet, I probably can't even do that without a few weeks' prep work first. Yep, I am one *hell* of a powerful supernatural.

I pass a woman with a hugely elaborate headdress and a forked tongue that darts out like a snake. A man in a sharp suit, with the build of a shifter, is talking to a naga, a benevolent serpent-like creature that normally favours rivers and other bodies of water. I've never heard of them taking human form.

A waiter passes me, holding a tray of champagne coupes. Or is it a waitress? I can't really tell. He or she has long straight hair that falls down their back over a loose, shapeless tunic and a weirdly blank face that's so pale, it's as if there's no blood beneath the skin. Their movements are wooden, like that of an automaton. And in fact, I can't see their chest rising and falling with their breath.

I realise what it is then, and recoil. A polong. A creature made by enchanting the blood of a victim who has been drained to their very last drop. The magic causes the blood to create a humanoid shape that lasts until the real body rots away to nothing. Polongs are deaf and blind and have no consciousness, save for the orders of their master. They're little more than puppets—animated objects.

I wonder if that means its master owns the Crane, which naturally brings me to the question, *who* is its master?

I turn away from the polong and realise that four people have stopped talking and are looking at me. They crowd together, the two women wearing opposite versions of red-and-black cheongsam, the two men wearing double-breasted suits that look like they were taken from Prohibition-era gangsters. The clothes aren't the most obvious similarities, though. Their yellowed, talon-like nails and surprisingly beautiful, feathery wings are far more noticeable than what they're wearing. They're mandurugo.

Vampires. Except that these guys don't bite their victims. And I'm facing four of them.

I arch an eyebrow, doing my best to ignore my sweaty palms and pounding heart. Those are the indicators of prey. "Anyone told you it's rude to stare?" I ask haughtily.

"And what's a little Mundane doing here tonight?" one of the women purrs. She's wearing the red dress with black detailing.

"Mundane? Piss off—you can tell I'm Touched."

"That makes no difference to us." One of the guys opens his mouth, and a pointed, tube-like tongue darts towards me.

I jump back, heart slamming in my chest like an addict pounding on a metal door for her fix. A shiver of fear and disgust runs through my spine.

Mandurugo don't bite their victims. They use their pointed tongues to pierce the skin and drink. Like the proboscis of a butterfly, if you can compare such a pretty creature to such foul beings as the mandurugo. Rumour has it, their favourites are pregnant women and foetuses. They are the embodiment of the word creepy, and the sight of that hideous tongue makes the skin all over my body crawl.

"I'm under Mr. Sangong's protection, and I'm here to see Sarroch," I warn them. "So you better leave me alone unless you think you can take them both on."

I'm hoping at least one of those names will impress.

Red laughs. "They'll just get another Mundane to replace you. Who can tell the difference between one Mundane and another anyway? Even when they *are* Touched..."

I reach out in panic, trying to sense for something, anything that could help. If I were like the rest of the Touched, I might have been able to send an SOS to Mr. Sangong or even to Chai, but I don't have that kind of range. And sending a message on my phone would require taking my attention off the mandurugo, which would be all kinds of stupid.

"And in any case," the woman in the black dress and red detail says. "Touched aren't allowed at the Crane. Punishment is required."

I smell blood on her breath, old blood, and rotten.

"I'm here to see Sarroch," I say loudly and forcefully, hoping someone else of importance will hear me. I take a step back, glancing around me, but no one's paying attention to us.

One man looks over at me but appears bored and returns to his conversation.

"I'm supposed to meet him in his private room. I've got important information I'm to deliver to him, and he won't be happy if you kill me before he can talk to me."

"Sarroch doesn't associate with trash," Red says.

"Well apparently he does." I'm too terrified to care that I've just admitted that I'm trash. "And you're scared to cross him, or you'd have attacked me by now." The moment I say the words, I realise they're true. I take a risk. "So either grow a pair and get on with draining me, or just let me pass."

I somehow find a way to look at them defiantly despite the sick knot of fear in my stomach. Did I really just challenge them to attack me?

And then a polong materialises at my side. This one has an actual midnight-blue uniform with brass buttons rather than the shapeless tunic of the waiters. It beckons for me to follow.

I raise an eyebrow at the mandurugo. "See?"

They glare at me balefully, but they part to let the polong lead me deeper into the main room. I almost groan with relief as we move out of the vampires' line of sight. Every one of my nerves is more coiled than my motorbike's suspension springs.

The polong leads me out of the main room and down a wide corridor. Lights gleam out from behind carved-wood panels that cast geometrical shadows on the marble floor. The polong makes no noise as it walks. Its feet are bare and as bloodless as its face, and yet they don't make the normal slapping-squeaky sound of skin against polished stone.

I don't know what part of the magic achieves that, nor do I care. My heart still hasn't slowed from my encounter with the mandurugo. The polong points to a half-open door then slips away down the corridor.

I take a deep breath. The evening hasn't even started, and I already feel exhausted and in waaaay over my head. Now I'm about to enter a meeting with an unknown magical creature, in a room without witnesses.

Sometimes I question my sanity.

I knock. "Sarroch?"

"You're late."

I roll my eyes. So much for a welcome. I push the door open and enter.

13

After the fear and the smell of rotten blood, the sight of Sarroch's private room feels jarring. It's all art nouveau and airy-fairy, with sinuous curves. One wall is covered with a huge mural of a wood nymph, her head crowned with flowers. She's nude other than a large, golden, sash-like ribbon coiling around her, not quite hiding the naughty bits. She's framed by a wreath of pale-green ferns, and she's wearing an expression that's probably designed to look pure and innocent but to me looks simpering.

Little green fairies with wings cavort, laughing, across another illustration hanging on the opposite wall, like some bad advert for absinthe. Speaking of which, there's a lacquered tray on top of a sideboard with all the tools to serve the liqueur. The bright-green stylised bottle of absinthe, a silver bowl full of brown sugar cubes, a silver slotted absinthe spoon, a cut crystal glass, and a carafe of water that's being kept cold through magic because although the room's a pleasant temperature, there's ice forming on the outside of the carafe.

The most ridiculous part about the decor, though, is that it was clearly done by a Mundane, following the Mundanes' ideas about dryads and fairies. The fairies are pale, pretty, with European features. Clearly whoever drew this has never seen a fairy for real, European *or* Asian. And don't get me started on the so-called nymph. If she's supposed to be a dryad, she should have tough, bark-like skin, yellow eyes, and hair like roots.

Dryads are *not* pretty.

On top of which, we don't get that kind of dryad here. Here our tree spirits are either orang bunian or pari-pari, so why the Crane displays a European Mundane's wet dream of a dryad is anyone's guess. On top of which, the pari-pari are far more beautiful.

I frown as something occurs to me, and I look over to where Sarroch is seated, looking relaxed. Is it a coincidence that I've been brought to a room with a wall featuring a European Mundane's equivalent of a pari-pari? Some kind of subtle message? It if is, it's too subtle for me to decipher.

Sarroch's looking at me, clearly not worried about being caught staring. His face is perfectly impassive. He hasn't changed since the office, although his shirt collar is wide open, and his eyes are darker. Full black, as if the pupils expanded until they took over the whole of the irises.

Behind him, an archway opens to a little boudoir-type space heaving with pale-green silk cushions. The boudoir looks pristine, and yet I get a sense that some serious debauchery has happened on those cushions. Not a useful insight, and I *especially* don't want to think about Sarroch in that kind of setting right now.

"Weird choice of décor." I arch an eyebrow and casually gesture at the room. It gives me something to do and buys me a precious few seconds to compose myself. Between the sight of the boudoir and the encounter with the mandurugo, I don't feel at my most poised.

"If I wanted your opinion on the décor, I'd have asked for it back when this place was being decorated, but you didn't *exist* back then."

Does that mean Sarroch is connected to the owner of the Crane? Or rather *is* he the owner? That would explain why the polong came to get me, if he controls them. My eyes drift to his hands, half expecting to see blood crusted around his fingernails, and I wonder how he drains the bodies required to make polongs.

Sarroch looks me over. "I'd have also expected a minimum of effort on the clothing front before you came to the Crane. You're not doing much to help the reputation of the Touched. Sangong is growing slack."

I shrug. This at least is familiar territory, and I've long ago stopped caring about what people think of my appearance. "Mr. Sangong knows what I'm like and accepts me as I am."

"Touching. Had I known this was how you would come, I'd have demanded you dress up for tonight." His eyes rest on my boots, and he shakes his head slightly.

I shrug. "I only dress up for *special* occasions, and a meeting with you certainly doesn't qualify." I grab myself a chair, relieved that the air of formality from the office is gone. I'm not sure if Sarroch is the one who broke that ice or if it's just a leftover from all the adrenaline I had pumping through my system a few moments ago with the mandurugo. Either way I'm really not in the mood to dance around the subject in the name of allowing someone to save face. "Now that the pleasantries are over, can we get this over and done with? I don't particularly enjoy getting threatened by mandurugo, so I'd like to get out of here as soon as I can."

Sarroch lowered his lids a little, hooding his eyes. Something about his gaze feels reptilian. "You have the egg?"

"You know I have." I grab the strap of my cross-body bag again. I'm still not lying, but I'm letting Sarroch come to the wrong conclusion about what's in the bag. "As I mentioned back at your office, Mr. Sangong said you could help me send it to a safe place. Can you?"

"Where did they want you to send the egg? The pari-pari?"

He didn't reply to my question, so I do the same. "They said it wasn't safe here in Panong. Do you know what that's about?" Sarroch doesn't need to know about the pari-pari's London relatives. Something else to look into—how on earth pari-pari exist in a city as busy as London.

Sarroch steeples his fingers, elbows resting on the curved armrests of his chair. "We're entering turbulent times."

"We are? Why?"

"We, the Mayak."

"Meaning it doesn't concern me? Turbulent times will affect me as much as everyone."

"That's true."

"So, what's causing these turbulent times?"

Sarroch considers me for a heartbeat, his eyes twin, unreadable black pools. I'm irritated to realise that once again, I'm noticing how handsome he is.

"The Mundanes," he says at last.

I frown. That was the last thing I expected. Mayak consider Mundanes to be barely a cut above cattle. How could the Mundanes be creating problems for the Mayak?

Sarroch seems to come to a decision and straightens up.

"All right, I'll arrange the shipping if you hand over the address and the egg."

"Are you having a laugh? You expect me to hand over the egg without knowing anything real about you, without knowing how you plan to ship it? Do you think I'm an idiot? I'm staying with the egg until it reaches its destination." I hadn't planned on that, but now that I've said it, I know it's true. Poor little mite—I'm not going to abandon it, not until I know it's safe. And one thing my gut's telling me is that it wouldn't be safe with Sarroch.

"If you weren't prepared to accept my help, then why did you come to my office earlier today?" he asks with obvious irritation.

"I came today because Mr. Sangong sent me and told me you could help. Help doesn't mean take over. I'm in charge of the egg, and I'm not about to just hand it over. I need a lot more before trust is established."

"I've been recommended by *Mr. Sangong*. That should be enough for the likes of you."

"The likes of me? What a fine job you're doing at changing my mind about you."

A flicker passes in Sarroch's eyes, as if something in his peripheral vision caught his attention, and he darts towards me with preternatural speed, snatching my wrist before I can react. "Give me the egg," he says aggressively, eyes boring into mine. His voice is low, too low. Menacing. "*Give it to me.*"

I see those flecks of gold in his eyes. Again, I feel like I'm falling, falling…

Somehow, I only just manage to pull myself back. My blood is pounding in my ears. What is he doing to me?

He's still holding my wrist when the door opens.

14

Pale, glamorous, impossibly beautiful. I blink at the woman standing in the doorway. She's wearing a shimmering white and gold dress from the thirties that's cut like a dream, but when she smiles, her teeth are sharp as a nightmare.

"Well, this looks cosy." Her voice is a mix of music and diamonds.

Her black fur coat has slipped down to her elbows, showing creamy white shoulders, and in one hand, she holds a long cigarette holder, the smoke coiling up to the ceiling. Her nails are vermillion and sharpened to talons.

"Why is a *Touched* dirtying the furniture?" This time her voice is cold enough to freeze and crack steel.

"Yue." Sarroch releases me and leans back in his chair. His manner is equally as cold. "I don't recall inviting you."

Yue shrugs and comes towards us. She folds herself expertly into a chair. She moves like something from a movie. "What is this intimate gathering in honour of? Playing with your food before you have a snack? I thought you found that to be bad manners."

The way she says this, glancing casually at her nails, makes me think that Sarroch has levelled this accusation at her before. I don't want to know how she hunts Mundanes because all the warning shivers are going off down the back of my neck right now. Whatever kind of creature she is, it's nasty.

I feel like a mouse who has just stumbled into the presence of an eagle.

"We're having a business discussion, Yue." Sarroch sounds irritated.

She laughs, the sound like tinkling silver bells. "With a Touched? And one who looks like *that*? What business could you *possibly* have with her?"

"I'm going to go," I say.

"No, no, no—this is clearly something interesting." Yue smiles, teeth glittering hard. "You will stay, and you will tell me just what exactly this business is about."

"I don't have to answer to you," I tell her coldly. "And if I want to go, then I will. Clearly, tonight was a complete waste of time, so..."

I'm about to stand up when her head turns slowly towards me, as if swivelling of its own accord atop her long, graceful neck. Her eyes are black as beetles, and I feel an odd prickling sensation on my skin.

She's doing something, although I have no idea what. I reach out with my pathetic little defences, doing my best to try and block it, but I find nothing to block.

"Apiya?" Sarroch's voice sounds distant, muffled. The room seems to have grown darker, too, the darkness crowding the edges of my vision.

My skin grows hot, uncomfortably so. My throat constricts, as if from an allergic reaction, and I'm finding it hard to breathe. I push harder, searching for Yue's energy, but it's as if she's doing nothing more than just looking at me.

"Apiya!"

I start to choke.

"Enough!"

I take a deep, ragged breath as air suddenly rushes into my lungs then cough a few times.

Sarroch is glaring at Yue. "What did you do?"

"Did you *sense* me do anything?" she asks innocently.

I'm still struggling to catch my breath, but the implication stops me cold. Yue did whatever she did without Sarroch sensing it, while he was right there and knew she was doing something? She's powerful indeed... and I need to get out of here fast. Sarroch is no protection, and something tells me Yue wouldn't mind feeding on a Touched tonight.

"I'm leaving." I stand uncertainly. My voice sounds hoarse.

Yue flicks ash from the tip of her cigarette onto the floor, and I feel the ridiculous urge to sweep it up. The smoke coils up to the ceiling. "Running back to your master?" she mocks. "Maybe you can do something for me, then. Give Sangong a message."

"You want to talk to him, you deliver your own damn message."

"All right, maybe I will. Then you can look forward to my visit at the barbershop."

I feel a spike of fear, and Yue smiles widely. She saw it.

"Leave her be," Sarroch snaps. "Why do you always have to do this, Yue?"

"Why else? Because I can."

———

SARROCH ARRANGES FOR A POLONG TO ESCORT ME OUT, BUT I'm in such a hurry to leave, it's struggling to keep up with me, given its slow and wooden movements.

This time I don't waste any time trying to make my way discreetly through the crowd. I shove my way through to a chorus of "Hey!" and "Watch it!"

What had felt like perfume from all the magic in the air now feels cloying and suffocating. The buzzing against my skin makes me feel raw. I'm scared, tired, and I just want out as fast as I can.

By the time I stagger outside, I'm desperate for fresh air, and I take deep, ragged breaths, gulping the night's cool humidity, leaning against the concrete wall next to the door.

The door guardians briefly materialise on the doors, check on me, then disappear again. I clutch at the strap of my cross-body bag with both hands, waiting for my breathing to slow and my heart to calm down.

Chai had had the right of it. This place is nasty and dangerous and really no place for someone like me. After he kept me so sheltered for years, I can't believe Mr. Sangong let me come here alone tonight. It makes no sense.

When I finally feel ready, I peel myself from the wall and head to my motorbike. I'm fiddling with the chain that keeps my helmet locked to the bike when I hear the scuffing of shoes against the ground behind me.

I drop the helmet and spin around.

"Hello again." It's one of the male mandurugo from earlier.

In fact, all four of them surround me, the two women in particular eyeing me hungrily.

"Your bag," the male orders, holding out his hand.

A coil of ice takes residence in my belly. They're here for

the egg. Sarroch must have sent them to get it from me after I left. Probably wanted to get it without Yue seeing.

"Your bag," the female echoes with a purr. "And then your blood."

15

I dig slowly into the bag, grabbing my razors. Then I fling it as far as I can to the side, flicking my razors open. Two of the mandurugo immediately rush to it, leaving me to face the other two.

I send out the loudest, strongest call for help I can manage, hoping that someone—Mr. Sangong, Chai—will sense it. I'm not holding my breath, though. My range isn't great.

My bike's of no use, either—I hadn't gotten around to removing the disc lock from the front wheel.

I shift my weight to the balls of my feet, bouncing lightly, arms loose, waiting as the male approaches me, waiting for him to come into range. He's the slightly shorter of the two.

I swing a *Te Tat* kick, a roundhouse kick that strikes with the lower part of the shin.

I'd gambled that mandurugo wouldn't be used to humans fighting back, so Shorty wouldn't be prepared to block.

The speed and power generated by the kick combined

with the heaviness of my boot means the kick lands with a satisfying crunch of broken ribs. I feel a distant flare of pain against my shinbone from the impact, but I'm well used to it from years of kicking this way.

Shorty falls from the impact. Not enough to injure him properly—he'll heal very quickly—but enough to buy me some time.

Unlike most other fighting styles, Muay Thai kicks land the fighter back in fighting position, so I bounce on my feet, turning towards the female—Red.

Just in time.

She's rushing me, moving with preternatural speed. I slash with matching speed. I've brought my magical razors, which enhance my speed and precision. Razors are much, much thinner blades than knives, so I won't be able to make any deep cuts.

But a nick at the right place, or rather at the wrong place, can be far more debilitating than a deep flesh wound. My left razor neatly slices her jugular open, enough to stop her. A quick *Teep Top* kick, a front thrust kick, drives her back, knocking her slightly off balance. Her nails gouged my left forearm, but nothing worrying. I send another call for help.

Red recovers fast and pounces on me again. Kicking to keep her at bay, and using my razors when she gets close to me, I only just manage to keep her off me.

Just.

The extra speed my razors give me is barely enough to match me to her speed. Lucky for me, mandurugo aren't that strong, so my kicks have serious impact.

A *Tae Chiang* kick makes her stumble to the floor, one leg out. A perfect opportunity. I jump and stomp on it with all my strength, breaking it.

The moment the bone breaks, I realise the mistake I've made. All this time I'd kept my motorbike at my back, as a small but important safety. In going after Red, I left the motorbike.

Hands grab me from behind.

I'm thrown on the floor, landing heavily on my back. Air whooshes out of my lungs.

I don't try to get my breath back. Years of training to get out of a vulnerable ground position has my body working on autopilot. Lungs burning, I throw my leg in the air in a kick that catches the face of the male mandurugo coming down at me.

My arms arc out with the magical razors to create a space for myself. I only barely miss a face, cutting hair instead.

I have just enough breathing room to get myself on one knee, crouching in tiger position.

The first two mandurugo are already recovering.

I kick out as Shorty rushes me, throwing my leg high enough to catch him in the groin with the heavy tip of my boot. It doesn't have the same impact as on a human. Mandurugo don't have much going on down there. Nothing in fact—they reproduce differently from us.

I use the recovery time from the low kick to spring up to a stand, but one of the females screams behind me, raking her nails across my face, making me cry out in pain as she slices the skin open.

I reach back with my razors and cut at her arms. She releases me.

Two mandurugo pounce on me, pinning me back on the floor. Red is straddling my chest. She pins my arms to the ground with her knees. My razors are useless.

"Oh, I'm going to enjoy draining you." Red opens her

mouth, her long, proboscis-like tongue stretching its hard tip towards me.

I thrash and buck, but she and the taller male with slicked-back hair have got me as pinned as a butterfly in a display case.

The female with the black dress and red detail kicks the right side of my face, and stars explode in my vision. I fall slack for a moment. Lucky for me, she's wearing soft leather pumps, or that could have been much, much worse.

Red laughs and lowers her head. I feel the tip of her tongue reach the side of my neck, right where my jugular is.

The stench of rotten blood is overwhelming.

"Wait!" I scream. "Wait! What about the egg?"

I'm not about to give it up, but I need something, anything, to buy me time.

"She's right, we need the egg," Slick Back says.

Red pouts, pulling back. "No fun."

I could weep with relief.

"Or we part drain her," Black suggests, grinning. "*Then* we get the egg."

"You know Mundanes can't function with only half their blood," Slick Back says.

"She's not a Mundane. She's Touched," Black says.

"Same same," Slick Back replies.

Shorty walks over to us, already recovering from his broken ribs. "*I'll* take a drink, so she knows we mean business, then she'll take us to the egg."

"Yes," Red purrs. She turns to me. "Give us the egg, and we'll consider letting you live."

"No!" I shake my head from side to side as Shorty knees down next to me.

The idea of any of them drinking from me makes me sick with terror.

Slick Back opens his mouth, tongue extending. I scream in fear with both my voice and senses.

But the night is dark and silent, swallowing my cries.

16

Slick Back's tongue reaches my neck, and I feel a sharp pain, like a needle being poked into a vein. Then my body goes completely slack, as if it fell asleep, but I'm still awake.

I can feel a pulling at my neck. I can see the stars in the sky overhead. I can hear low laughter around me.

And then sensation comes rushing over me, wrenching me out of my near-comatose state. Loud barking rings out in the night. Barking I'd recognise anywhere.

Hunter.

I reach for him, and everything grows confused.

Hunter slams into Slick Back, knocking the mandurugo off me. Screams rise up with the barking. Too much sensation rushes over me, and I can't make sense of it. Movement, sound, taste, smell...

I'm trying to get up, but I'm as weak as a newborn. I'm aware of Hunter biting something hard—somehow I can feel the hardness beneath his teeth.

I get to my feet, legs shaking beneath me, the world swaying dangerously.

I hear the gut-wrenching sound of Hunter yelping in pain. "Hunter, no! What—"

Something crashes into me from the back, and the world goes dark.

———

I COME TO, BLINKING SLOWLY. YELLOW LIGHT. I'M LYING ON something soft. The inside of my mouth feels tacky and tastes metallic.

I blink again.

There's a bloody fairy on the ceiling. A European fairy. One of the idiotic, pretty renditions Mundanes are so fond of.

Then everything comes crashing back to me. "Hunter!" I sit bolt upright and nearly topple sideways. Everything hurts, and everything around me feels like it's moving in ways it shouldn't. I only just manage to stop myself from throwing up.

"Slowly, you need to give it time to take effect."

I'm back in Sarroch's private room at the Crane, and he's sitting in the same chair as before, this time angled to face me. I'm in the boudoir with the pale-green cushions.

"Time for what to take effect?" I've got the mother of all headaches. "Where's my dog?"

"The blood."

"What blood? Who's blood? How long was I out? Where's Hunter?"

"Just under an hour. Who's Hunter?"

I pull myself to a stand, teeth gritted. I've sprained my left ankle, which forces me to lean my bodyweight on my right foot. My head is pounding like my brain is trying to break through my skull. My right shoulder has been swallowed by a low throb, and my face feels like it was shredded to ribbons. Which, I suppose, it was.

"Hunter's my dog. Where is he?"

Sarroch comes to stand next to me and takes my elbow. His grip is so firm it's just shy of painful. "You should sit back down. You're still too weak."

I attempt to yank my arm out of his grip, but it's my right arm, and I barely manage a feeble movement before the pain in my shoulder has me wincing and stumbling.

"That was unnecessary," Sarroch says reproachfully.

I turn and look at him coldly. "I almost died, so excuse me if I don't feel like repeating the experience. Let *go* of me."

He does. "The mandurugo attack was unfortunate, but you're fine."

"Unfortunate? Fine? Do I *look* fine to you?"

"You'll be in a much worse state if you don't give up the egg."

"Are you threatening me?"

"No, just making you aware of your reality."

"Prat off."

Sarroch frowns. "What?"

"Er—English insult. It doesn't translate well in Panongian. I meant to say piss off."

Sarroch steps up to me, crowding my personal space, looming over me. I try to move away, but I'm too slow. He's quite a bit taller than I am, and I have to look up to meet his eyes. He's so close I can smell him—musk and something spicy-smoky, like dried tobacco and cinnamon.

He takes both my elbows. "Give me the egg." His voice is so deep I feel it rumble in my ribcage. His eyes are infinite pools in inky darkness. Flickers of gold appear in their depths. "Give me the egg now. Take me to it."

I'm falling, falling... my face is tingling. "I...I..."

"Take me to the egg, Apiya!" His voice is loud, and I feel a spike of fear.

An image materialises in my mind then. Hunter. It's more than an image. It's like, for a moment, my senses are full of him.

Hunter, out there, alone. Hurt. Whatever Sarroch is doing collapses before the onslaught of Hunter, the urgency of finding him replacing all else.

"Get off me," I snarl.

Sarroch frowns, a hint of surprise in his eyes.

I stagger away, relieved when he doesn't try to stop me. I throw myself at the door, nearly fall over as I open it, and stumble out into the corridor.

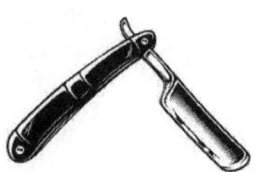

17

Outside there's no sign of Hunter. I don't know whether to be panicked or relieved. If he's not here, that means he was able to get away, which means he's alive.

But he's hurt. I heard it, and what's more confusing—and I'm really not in the right frame of mind to think about it right now—I felt it in some way I haven't experienced before.

The thought of my darling boy out in the dark somewhere all alone and hurt makes it hard to breathe.

"Hunter!" I yell at the top of my voice. He never comes when I call, but maybe if he hears me, I'll get at least some kind of reaction that can point me towards him. "Hunter!"

I reach the spot where the fighting took place. My bag is still there, its contents scattered on the ground. My motorbike's been knocked over—not that I care. There's blood on the ground.

Mine? I swallow. Hunter's?

"Hunter!"

Then I hear it, faint but unmistakable, a whine.

I limp as fast as I can in its direction, continuing to call Hunter's name. He whines again, a weak, mournful sound. "I'm coming, my darling. I'm coming!"

I head into the forest, crashing clumsily through the undergrowth. It doesn't take me long to find him lying next to a small river. He lifts his head and thumps his tail once, but he doesn't get up. I can see his chest fluttering rapidly, and there's blood in his fur around his stomach. He still has his leash on, and it trails behind him on the ground.

It's all I can do not to break down sobbing. I kneel at Hunter's side, hands shaking, oh so close to giving in to panic. I need to get him help. I need a vet. I need—all I have is a motorbike, and there's no way I can ride it and carry him at the same time.

I could try to sense out for Mr. Sangong in the hope that he would realise my emergency, but that hasn't worked so far. Then I curse as I realise my stupidity—I'm focusing on magic here when technology would be a far better option.

"I'll be right back, Hunter. You be a good boy and stay here. I'll be right back!"

The pain in my ankle fades in front of the emergency, and I sprint back to where the mandurugo emptied my bag. I quickly find my phone. The screen is cracked, but I'm finally having some luck—it still works.

I call Chai.

"Api! I was so worried. Hunter—"

"Is here. He's hurt. Badly. I need a car. I need a vet. I need a healer. Now. Yesterday."

"On it. What happened. Is he...?"

"He's bleeding, and—" I find I can't go on, and breaking down into sobs over the phone isn't going to help.

I describe how to find us from the Crane and hang up

after Chai promises he'll be here as soon as he can. And I know that when he needs to drive fast, he's *fast*.

I grab one of my razors and rush back to Hunter's side, throw off my leather jacket, and strip off my top, cutting it into thick strips in the hope of using it as a makeshift bandage. I try to identify where the wound is exactly, and Hunter whimpers. I try to move him to apply the bandage, and he yelps in pain.

"You should leave him be," a male voice says.

Only the desire not to hurt Hunter any further stops me from jumping right out of my skin.

A pari-pari is crouching by the river's edge. His eyes are wide and sorrowful as he looks at Hunter. His skin is mottled in various shades of grey and blue, like water rushing over stones. His teeth are the colour of moss, and he has no wings.

Something about him speaks of age, of centuries past. A sense of dark places and the immutable power of water rolls off him. Power that can maybe help us.

"Can you heal him?" I beg. "Please."

The pari-pari shakes his head sadly. "He's dying. There's nothing I can do."

"No," I say forcefully. "No, he just needs healing. He—you're wrong."

The pari-pari shakes his head again. I feel an irrational rush of anger at him and all of his kind—if not for that damn egg...

"They gave you their egg," he says slowly, with wonder.

I recoil. "You hear thoughts?"

"No. I was sensing you, and I can tell you had contact with an egg recently. It's a mark of enormous respect from my people to have entrusted you with an offspring."

"Why was I given it? Why me? Why wasn't it safe for the egg to stay with its parents?"

"I can't answer any of that without revealing some of my people's secrets—the knowledge of those secrets is the very thing that now threatens our safety. You must get the egg away from here, far away. Our people's survival depends on it."

"And how do you expect someone like me to handle this when I don't even know how to look after the damned egg?"

"So long as you take care of it, it will be fine."

For a moment, I'm not sure if the pari-pari is mocking me, repeating Mr. Sangong's words.

"Any way of looking after the egg is fine," he adds gently. "So long as care is taken over it."

I hear the sound of a car arriving, and my head snaps sideways. A door opens and closes. "Chai? Chai! Over here!"

He reaches my side a couple of moments later and gasps at the sight of Hunter. My stomach sinks—he's alone. No vet and no healer.

"I called every vet I could on the drive over, but nothing is open this late. I only know of one healer, but I couldn't get through to her. I called ten times."

I glance back at the old pari-pari, but he's disappeared. He wasn't right about Hunter—I won't let him be right.

"Help me move Hunter," I tell Chai. "We're taking him to the barbershop."

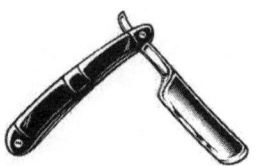

18

Moving Hunter is an ordeal. Thankfully Chai's calm manner helps soothe my anxiety a little. He helps me pick Hunter up, which makes him whimper and whine with pain. I'm crying like an open faucet as we bring him to Chai's car.

The car's a custom job Chai made himself, and it runs fast. Very fast. Right now, that's what we need.

Chai sends us roaring into the night in a screech of tyres that leave rubber on the tarmac.

I stay in the back seat, cradling Hunter's head, whispering words of reassurance, stroking his ears. "You'll be fine, my darling. I'm here. You'll be fine."

By the time we reach the barbershop, I've stopped crying, but I still feel so tense I could be snapped in half like a twig.

"Tim!" I bellow as we enter.

The cat comes sauntering out of the office. "What's with the commotion—no! That dog's not allowed in the barbershop! It's minging, it stinks. Also, Apiya, you look like hell."

"Send word to Mr. Sangong that there's an emergency and he needs to come to the barbershop now."

Tim sits on his haunches, wrapping his tail neatly around his paws. "I can't do that—"

"Bullshit. You've been with Mr. Sangong long enough. We're in his territory, so you can feed off his magic. You can figure out how to get to him if it's really important."

"A *dog's* important?"

I move with more speed than I'd have expected of myself given the state I'm in and scoop him up so I can hold him at face level. "Tim, I've never asked you for anything real, but I am now. You *have* to get Mr. Sangong here. I don't know what I'll do if..." My voice breaks, my face scrunching up as the tears come, which makes the cuts sting like hell.

"All right, all right, love," Tim mutters. "No need to get all up in my face about it. I was only joking. I can contact Mr. Sangong for emergencies."

I set him back on the ground, and he lies down, paws tucked neatly under himself, eyes closing.

"Seriously, Tim! Emergency!" I snap my fingers in his face.

He cracks an eye open, giving me a very catlike glance of contempt. "Can it, treacle. It takes concentration and skill to summon Mr. Sangong, so stop distracting me."

"Petal, maybe you should come sit next to Hunter," Chai says to me in a low, soothing voice, gently taking my elbow. "Freaking out and running about the place is not going to achieve anything. Are you cold? Do you need clothes?"

"Huh?" I realise I'm still only wearing my cropped sport brassière. "I'm fine."

I sit by Hunter's side, stroking his head and flank. "Hold on just a little longer. Until Mr. Sangong gets here."

"Apiya! Are you all right?"

I jump to my feet at the sound of his voice. Mr. Sangong is walking in through the door. Tim is obviously more effective than he appears, and Mr. Sangong must have materialised or teleported—it doesn't matter.

He's here.

"Hunter is dying. You have to do something. He saved my life after I was attacked outside the Crane. I was attacked by mandurugo. Hunter is bleeding all over—his stomach... You have to do something." I'm babbling, the words pouring out of me in a torrent.

Mr. Sangong frowns and looks over at Hunter. "It's too late, Apiya," he says gently. "Hunter is dying—"

"*No.* You have to fix this. *You* sent me to Sarroch, and *he* was behind the attack."

Mr. Sangong raises an eyebrow in surprise. "My powers aren't limitless."

"Then get someone here who can do something. There are necromancers out there, for crying out loud. I know there are Mayak who can stop death."

Mr. Sangong cocks his head, considering me.

"What? Why are you looking at me instead of doing something?" I'm teetering oh so close to the edge of hysterical.

"It's a *dog*," he replies slowly.

And there I go, plunging waaaaaay past the edge of hysterical. "*You* sent me to Sarroch!" I don't care that I just sprayed him with spittle. "*You* left me to go to the Crane on my own. I messaged you several times about getting backup, about whether I'd be safe to go, and you never bothered to reply. I nearly *died* because you can't figure out how to work a bloody mobile phone! Hunter saved me. *You* made a mistake in sending me to Sarroch. *You* made a mistake in not replying to me about the Crane, and Hunter cleared *your* mess for you. You owe him. You owe him, and if you don't heal him *right now*, I... I..."

The wave of rage breaks, disappearing as abruptly as it came, and without its burning energy, I'm struggling to think, let alone talk.

Mr. Sangong comes to my side and puts a hand on my shoulder. "This is really important to you." Mr. Sangong is looking at me intently.

I make a squeak in the affirmative. I can't put into words how important Hunter is, but he is. He really is.

"All right. I do not normally do this. I do not dance with death."

"Just one t-time. Please," I whisper.

"I will need to use your connection to Hunter. Put your hands on him and focus."

My legs wobble from the sheer power of the relief washing over me. Chai has to catch me by the elbow, or I'd have fallen on my face like a puppet with cut strings.

"Keep your focus on Hunter," Mr. Sangong instructs as I put one hand on Hunter's head and one hand on his flank.

He's barely breathing.

I close my eyes and concentrate. I hear Mr. Sangong take a breath, and all of a sudden, the quality of the air changes. That feeling of licking a battery rises up, like an electrical buzzing in the air. He hasn't done or said anything, and yet everything feels different. Something breaks in a tinkling of glass, and the light dims a little—a lightbulb. Then Mr. Sangong begins to whisper sounds that should be impossible for a human tongue to make.

19

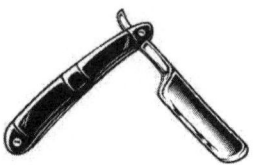

Everything becomes confused after that. I'm not really aware of anything other than the feel of Hunter beneath my hands. It briefly feels like an enormous amount of energy is whirling around me, passing through me, and that's the last clear thing I remember.

I come to, blinking and groggy, in my own bed. Everything hurts—and I do mean *everything*. A full body ache, as if I've run several triathlons followed by a mammoth Muay Thai sparring session. I roll to my side, and something crinkles against my cheek.

It's a note, and I extract it from under my face and bring it up to eye level. Chai's neat handwriting.

Good morning, princess. I've gone home for a shower and change and to grab a couple hours of shut-eye. Hunter is awake. He's fine and waiting to give you a big slobbery kiss.

PS: I went to get your motorbike and your bag.

PPS: last night, I told Hunter that if he pulled through, I would lift my ban on slobber. I think that's what made all the difference. You're welcome.

Right now, I don't think I can put into words how much I love Chai.

But first things first. I toss the note aside and sit up with all the speed and agility of a ninety-year-old geriatric. "Hunter?" I croak.

I hear a loud rustling coming from the living room. I clamber awkwardly out of bed and walk out of the bedroom.

Hunter has managed to open the cupboard in which I keep his kibble—I bulk buy enormous bags, so it works out cheaper. He's dragged the open bag onto the sofa, and as I walk into the living room, he's in the process of inserting the top half of his body into the bag.

The bag is almost empty, so he's having to go deep into it. But he's obviously not thought the idea through because he panics, shaking his head from side to side, and as he does, he loses his footing and tumbles off the sofa in a tangled mess, kibble flying everywhere.

I limp over, laughing, and yank the bag off him. That is the best confirmation that Hunter is doing fine.

I'm expecting an emotion charged, or at least excited reunion, but there's kibble on the floor, so Hunter barely acknowledges me, rushing to hoover up as much of the food as he can. I do my best to run my hands along his belly, feeling for the wound, but there's nothing but smooth, furry skin. As if he's never been injured.

The relief is overwhelming. I awkwardly cuddle his back as he chomps on the kibble, needing that contact with him for a moment. He's healed. Truly, properly healed.

"Thank you," I tell Mr. Sangong, even though he can't hear.

I'll thank him properly later and maybe apologise for how I spoke to him. Although I still stand by some of what I said. If he wasn't so useless at replying to messages, if he'd come with me to the Crane, if he hadn't sent me to Sarroch, the mandurugo attack might never have happened, and Hunter wouldn't have gotten hurt.

On that note... at some point, I'll need to figure out what happened exactly that Hunter, who has never once come when I call him, crossed a significant portion of town to get to me when I wasn't even calling him using voice.

One thing at a time, though. For now, shower.

I give Hunter a final squeeze and a kiss on top of his velvet head, but he wriggles away from me, continuing his hunt for the kibble. My dog adores me... unless there's food present. I know my place in the pecking order, and we're clearly back to business as normal. Something settles inside me, like a deep exhale after a long period of holding my breath.

I leave Hunter to stalk his kibble and head to the bathroom.

Tim had the right of it last night—I look like hell. My left eye is red and puffy, probably from all the crying and from exhaustion. My right eye is a little swollen and surrounded by ugly purple bruising. The cuts across my face have scabbed over, but the sight of them makes me wince. The mandurugo who clawed at my face wasn't messing about.

I shudder at the memory of how close things got. With nails that sharp, given the chance, the mandurugo could have done much more serious damage. My right shoulder is also heavily bruised, but it doesn't take me long to establish that it's nothing serious. No punching or sparring for me for a while, though. As to my rolled ankle, I'll wrap it, and it should be fine in a couple of days.

I inspect my neck where the male mandurugo had begun to drink my blood, but there's nothing, not so much as a scratch. A shiver of revulsion goes through me at the memory of that sharp, tube-like tongue stretching towards me.

And then there's the matter of the blood I was fed. If my stomach wasn't already empty, I would probably be heaving up its contents right now.

I jump in the shower, needing to wash off the night's events. I shower until the hot water runs out and continue for a while longer with cold water.

* * *

Once I finally feel clean, I go and check on the menagerie. Fergie has gotten himself wedged in an empty flowerpot. My guinea pig squeaks "lettuce" at me—in short, all is as it should be.

I put on a Louis Armstrong record—the record player is another one of my improvements, like what I did for the one at the barbershop. I need a beat of normality, of pottering around the house and doing chores. It's soothing after last night's events, and it gives me time to ground myself. Otherwise given half the chance, too many thoughts would take over and whirl inside my mind.

Plus, I love my little house, and I love to keep it clean. It's a tiny traditional house in Old Town, no bigger than a regular one bedroom apartment, really—just split over two floors and with a courtyard.

When I moved, it was uninhabitable—you couldn't even use it for storage, let alone to live in it. Mould was growing on the walls, there were more leaks than I could count, and many of the floor tiles were broken...As a result, the rent I pay on it is less than nothing, even though it has an outdoor space.

But as I mentioned before, this is one of the few areas where my magic is actually useful. It took me some time to get to know the place, but as it got familiar with me, things started to cooperate. The mould disappeared, the leaks took care of themselves, and with new tiles to replace the broken ones, it's become a lovely home.

All my furniture is like that as well—trash that people threw out, that I've fixed and transformed and improved. Sometimes I think I can feel gratitude from my furniture at having been rescued, but that's probably my imagination.

I grab my cross-body bag, which is hanging from the back of a chair, and I'm about to put it away when I notice a blue glow coming from within it. I open it to find the pari-pari egg inside.

I frown, temporarily confused. Then flashes of memory from the previous night come back to me. I remember Mr. Sangong telling me that if Hunter survives the night, he will be fine. I remember going to get the egg from the office and lying down on the floor with Hunter and the egg—for some reason it seemed like having the egg nearby would help Hunter, although I have no idea what made me think that. And I remember Chai bringing me home. He's surprisingly strong despite his slim build.

I glance over at my dog, who's still enthusiastically snuffling around the sofa, trying to get the last remaining kibble from under it. Does he even remember last night?

I fish out the egg from the bag. It still feels warm, its blue light pulsing gently. I need to find a safe place for it—safe and warm.

I briefly consider tucking it away in one of my clothes drawers, but that feels lonely, not to mention unsafe. Now that I truly do have the egg, what's to stop Sarroch from sending goons to break into my place?

Plus my gut tells me that closeness with animals is a good idea. After all, normally the egg would be reared around other pari-pari, in nature.

I go outside, to the rabbits' hutch. There's a false bottom that I had built in. I've *suggested* to the hutch and the rabbits that the droppings should roll to the edges of the hutch, where a narrow gap allows them to fall into the compartment below rather than just stay in the hutch. That means I can empty out the tray beneath the false bottom daily, and it keeps the hutch much cleaner.

The compartment is just about deep enough for the egg, and I stuff the space with straw to stop the egg from rolling around but also to make it comfortable. My guinea pig enthusiastically squeaks "lettuce" at me, so I give him a few leaves and some carrot peelings—his favourite, even though he still only asks for lettuce. I think he doesn't know the difference between the words lettuce and food.

I'm washing my hands when my phone rings—it's my dad. It's four p.m. here, so with the time difference, it's morning in England.

I answer the video call but block my camera. I don't want him to see my messed-up face. The video on his side is barely better, showing me a close-up of his nostrils.

"Dad, move the phone. I can't see your face."

"Apiya!" he yells. He understands audio only calls just fine, but for some reason, the moment video is involved, he has to shout loud enough to project his voice all the way from London to Panong. "I can't see you!"

"My camera's turned off."

The image sways dangerously. I hear muttered swearing, then I'm treated to a close-up of the inside of his ear.

"Dad, you might want to invest in some Q-tips."

"Apiya!" he shouts again. More swaying of the video then the screen goes dark.

Another successful call with my father. I call my mother and get her to put him on the phone, audio only this time.

"Oh, sweetheart," he says, "I'm glad to catch you. Those idiotic smartphones never work. The screen was black. I couldn't see anything..." He grouses on for a moment.

Picking your battles is important in life—I don't correct him about the phone.

"How are you?" I ask at the first opportunity I get to interrupt his complaining about phones.

"I have a source for you to get the information you want about pari-pari and their eggs."

"Ooh, tell me!"

"A young woman at Panong University with whom I have worked numerous times . She's a research assistant— her name is Ilmu. It took me a while to contact her because she's really terrible with technology. Not much common sense, you know."

"That's rich, coming from you."

Dad sniffs. "She's worse than me, I'll have you know. *And* she's younger."

"That could only be possible if she's Amish."

I hear laughter in the background.

Dad sighs. "The female sense of humour is the bane of my existence. Your mother made the same remark last night. Anyway, Ilmu got back to me saying she has the information you're after. She's very good at what she does, very thorough in her research. A bit weird, very awkward, incapable of working a computer, but amazing with old manuscripts."

"And you've known her for a while?"

"Years! In fact she's become my go-to for more obscure

information sources. Anything she tells you will be reliable unless she specifies otherwise."

"That's great. Thanks, Dad."

"Also, since getting ahold of her is so complicated, I told her you'd be around by the end of the day today. Otherwise it would have taken another few days to arrange an appointment. I hope that's okay."

My body protests at the thought of having to do anything other than lounge on the sofa. But last night was a very stark indicator that I need to know more if I'm to deal with the egg and not get killed in the process. I'm several trains behind everyone, and I need to catch up.

I message Chai to ask if he would mind coming to hang out with Hunter while I'm gone. The reply is instant and eager, not that I'm surprised. He briefly tries to get concerned for me, fussing like a mother hen, but I put a swift end to that. I don't need smothering. I need someone to watch my back, and there's no one I would rather have than Chai.

Getting up from the sofa causes my body to groan and ache, but I do my best to ignore it and get ready to ride.

20

I lmu's office is on the edge of Panong University's campus. Between Dad's directions and what I remember from when I studied here, I find my way without needing to ask anyone. That's just as well because my face is bound to attract attention and questions. As it is, I keep it hidden beneath my motorbike helmet.

I reach the door and remove my helmet, putting on a pair of sunglasses to hide my right eye with its burst blood vessels. That would gross out anyone, and I don't want to answer questions about it. I'm too tired to tell good lies and keep track of them. I knock.

"Come in!"

I enter a room that's so messy it makes my hands itch. There are papers everywhere, and I do mean *everywhere*. Where there aren't any papers, there are books. And covering all the papers and all the books is a nice thick layer of dust. The air conditioning unit has been set to blow warm air, making the room uncomfortably stuffy, and I'm immediately too hot in my riding leathers.

Looking half buried in the mound of paper, like a

hamster in its nest, is a woman I'm guessing is Ilmu, sitting behind a desk. She's a skinny Panongian with skin so pale it almost looks translucent. Her chin looks like it gave up the fight, kind of sloping down into her neck without ever really making an appearance. Her spine droops with the limpness of an old sock as she hunches over her desk. She's wearing a white T-shirt with a nineties strappy dress on top, and her bare arms have all the muscle tone of an overcooked noodle.

And speaking of socks, there is one on the chair that faces her desk. Not a clean sock that has fallen out of a laundry hamper. No. A *dirty* sock.

Ilmu blinks at me, her eyes magnified by a pair of glasses so thick they could have been used to build jam jars. Her hair is somehow messily piled atop her head, looking like a small rodent would be quite at home there. In fact, it's very meta. Her hair is a rodent's nest within the rodent's nest of her office.

Her features have that ageless quality, so I can't tell whether she's in her twenties or forties.

"Are you Apiya?"

"Top marks for you. My father said you were expecting me this afternoon."

The most interesting thing about Ilmu, though, is that I'm picking up magic from her. I don't think she's Touched. There's too much depth to what I can sense. Touched magic is unidimensional, and Ilmu definitely has several facets.

On top of which, now that I think of it, her office is in an obviously forgotten corner of the university at the end of a dead-end corridor. There are no other offices here—just store rooms and a toilet— clearly, people rarely come this way. Just the kind of place the Mayak like.

"Your dad said you were looking for information on the pari-pari? Please take a seat."

"There's a sock on your chair."

Ilmu straightens up and looks over at the chair with a frown. "So there is."

"Are you going to remove it?"

"You're closer to it."

"Physical proximity has nothing to do with it. This isn't my sock, and I'm not in the habit of handling other people's dirty laundry."

"Oh, I'm not expecting you to clean it. You can just put it on the floor."

Definitely Mayak. A Touched would have been embarrassed.

I'm sorely tempted to argue, but I need her to do me a favour. I reach towards the chair with my boot and use it to drag the offending sock to the floor. I look at the chair dubiously, suggesting it lets go of its dirt, but it fails to respond to my magic. Yet more evidence of the vastness of my power. Tremble and cower all thee who look upon me! I'll need several more visits before I can influence the chair.

"So, the pari-pari?" Ilmu asks.

I look away from the chair to meet her gaze, and I cross my arms. "You haven't made any comment or asked any questions about my face. Most people seeing scratches like mine would at least express surprise or curiosity. I look like some kind of animal attacked me."

"Did an animal attack you?"

I take a gamble. "A mandurugo." I stare at her in challenge.

Ilmu holds my gaze for a few heartbeats. "I heard about what happened at the Crane." Her tone is mild.

I guessed right. "So you're Mayak."

"I'd expect you to be able to sense that without me having to tell you, given that you're Touched."

Touché. "So why are you willing to give me information? The Mayak don't normally do the Touched any favours."

Ilmu shrugs. "The Mayak have cast me out, or as close as."

"Why?"

"That's my business."

"You'll have to do better than that. If you know what happened last night, you'll know I'm not in much of a trusting mood when it comes to the Mayak."

"You're asking me to do you a favour, remember?"

"I don't buy that. You wouldn't be doing this unless there's something in it for you as well."

"Suffice to say that I have no great loyalty to the Mayak, and I'm quite happy to help out the Touched."

I arch an eyebrow. "How do I know you're telling me the truth?"

Ilmu gives a thin smile. "If I show you my true form, it will give you a pretty good idea of why I've been cast out and why I can be trusted."

I narrow my eyes. "Seriously, what's in this for you? Why are you going so far to convince me I should let you do me a favour?"

Ilmu places her hands carefully on the desk. "I want to make sure the pari-pari egg doesn't end up in the wrong hands. We're in a delicate position as it is, and that egg could plunge the world into chaos. So yes, you are doing me a favour because I have a very big stake in ensuring large-scale destruction is averted."

I stumble backwards. "How the hell do you know about the egg?"

"Seriously? I've heard rumours of a new pari-pari egg, then all of a sudden, you happen to need information about eggs. What other conclusion should I come to, exactly?"

Okay, that *does* make sense.

Ilmu raises an eyebrow. "You're pretty slow for a Touched. I thought your kind had to be sharp to survive in the world of the Mayak. Now, if you give me a moment, I'll show you my true form."

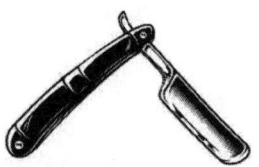

21

Ilmu steps away from her desk, finding a space to stand among all the mess. She looks as small and fragile as a hermit crab without its shell. Her dress is shapeless, reaching mid-calf. She's wearing shoes with an inch-think platform sole and white ankle socks. Her calves are like two little broomsticks poking out of the socks.

Then her glamour begins to ripple and fade. But it's not just the appearance of a nerdy young woman that disappears. It's the whole office. I've heard of, but never seen, creatures who have to glamour the space around them as well as themselves.

I find myself face to face with a huge beast on all fours and take a step back.

She has the head, tusks, and trunk of an elephant but with horns protruding from her forehead. The wrinkled grey elephant-like skin runs down to her torso, where it gives way to gleaming brown fur—the body of a bear. Black-and-orange stripes run from her shoulders to her haunches, and her claws are most definitely those of a tiger.

Along with the tusks, horns, and claws, the size of her

would have made her terrifying, but her posture—coy to the point of almost cringing—and her large, sad eyes make her appear like a shy, lumbering creature rather than a fearsome monster.

"You're a baku," I whisper in wonder.

The office has given way to a kind of library, stacks stretching out in all directions, disappearing into the gloom. I wonder if there's an end to them or if the baku occupies an unlimited space.

The stacks all have a base of red painted with golden symbols. But instead of containing books of paper, the stacks are full of ancient books made from bamboo slats. Each slat holds long columns of symbols, the slats sewn together. The resulting documents are all rolled up and kept in place by thick red ribbons.

The space feels ancient, the sheer amount of knowledge held in the bamboo books radiating out as clearly as magic. And yet there is no dust, and the air doesn't smell stale. Instead, it feels comfortable, as if there should be a plush reading chair and table with a glass of port on it.

My father would lose his mind with excitement if he knew this existed. My mum's joke would become reality— he'd dive into one of the stacks and would forget to ever reappear for air or food. I know baku are supposed to be benevolent, but that could just be a front to lure humans into getting lost within those stacks.

Much as I'd love to riffle through the bamboo books, I'm not about to touch anything unless I know exactly how this place operates.

"Please don't touch my memories," Ilmu says. Her voice is extremely deep, rumbling in that massive chest, but there's a softness to it.

"I thought bakus devoured nightmares."

"We do, but we consume other things as well."

"Memories?" I recoil.

"At the end of life, yes. Sometimes we consume memories given to us voluntarily in mid-life, although that can be... a little risky. It requires a great deal of self-control to stop in time."

I remember what she said about being cast out. "Did you consume the memory of a Mayak? The wrong Mayak? The wrong memory?"

The sad eyes look away. "That's for me to know. But I hope this has satisfied you."

The baku and her library shimmer and ripple, and a moment later, I'm back in the dusty office with the droopy-spined research assistant.

Well, my dad has come through, all right. Any information I need about the pari-pari, the baku is bound to know.

After a final inspection of the chair where the dirty sock had, until recently, resided, I take a seat so I'm facing Ilmu, now back in her own chair. "You said before that we're in a delicate position. Last night Sarroch told me that there were turbulent times coming. What's going on?"

"Is that really all Sarroch told you?"

"He said the Mundanes were behind the turbulence. But I don't see how that's possible... Mundanes are far too weak to cause trouble for the Mayak."

"Do you really believe that?" Ilmu raises an eyebrow at me, her expression and tone making it clear that I've just said something stupid.

I frown. "Your glamour strikes me as a lot more sarcastic than your true form."

"And your true form strikes me as lacking intelligence. Why do you think the use of tattoos has been banned for the Touched? You're far too close to the Mundanes. And that makes you a threat. The tattoos boost your powers, powers that could be turned against the Mayak if the Mundanes ever decide to rise up against us."

I snort. "The Mayak think of us much in the same way that a human would think about an insect, to say nothing of the Mundanes. I doubt they see us as a threat."

"The only reason insects aren't a threat to humans is because they mostly go about their business and haven't made it a priority to attack humans. A single human against a single ant isn't a contest. But what if all the insects that crawl underground and buzz in the sky suddenly united and attacked?"

I frown. "Even then, the Mayak have such powers..."

"We do. But there are only several hundred thousand of us. There are eight *billion* of you."

"Sure, but the Mundanes don't know about the Mayak's existence, at least not beyond fairy tales and ancient myths. Which is why they don't do anything."

"That's true, and that's why we've been able to coexist in peace all these centuries. But things are changing, and they have been for a few decades, now. Humans are slowly turning the world into one big shopping mall. The Crane can't exist in a shopping mall. Your barbershop can't exist in a shopping mall. The pari-pari, the orang bunian, and all the other forest folk need ancient forests to exist and to breed. Palm oil plantations are for them as sterile as a shopping mall is for us city dwellers. The Mundanes don't need to know about our existence to wipe us out. We're old creatures, and there is no space for us in the new world of internet and plastic the Mundanes are creating."

* * *

A tight knot has been forming in my belly as Ilmu speaks. I think of all the recent development in Panong—the new skyscrapers, the wider roads, the new influx of cars. And yes, there is a giant shopping mall currently being built on the edge of Old Town. "So, what does it mean? What's going to happen? You mentioned chaos before..."

Ilmu nods. "There are two schools of thought as to how we ensure our survival. One of them is to infiltrate the Mundane world and attempt to change it from the inside."

"And the other?"

"Destruction. Until there aren't enough Mundanes left to be a threat to us."

My mouth goes dry. And that's why the Touched are no longer allowed tattoos to boost their abilities. Given how marginalised we are from Mayak society, it doesn't take a genius to guess which way the Touched would side if it came to a war between Mundanes and Mayak.

"Where do you stand?" I ask.

Ilmu gives a sad smile. "Have you ever heard of an aggressive baku? We're creatures of stories and knowledge and memories. The Mundanes may be small and short-lived, rushing around and paying attention to all the wrong things, but they can be capable of great beauty, art, wonderful stories... to lose that would be tragic."

"What about the pari-pari egg? You said that it would be very dangerous for the egg to fall into the wrong hands."

"Do you understand how magic works? For the Touched and for the Mayak?"

I nod. The Mayak are, in essence, magic that has crystallised into solid beings. Through the process of crystallisation, some aspects of the magic are lost, which limits the beings' powers, and which is why different Mayak have different abilities.

The Touched, however, aren't made of magic but only touched by it, so they have a single-focus type of magic. They can work with a single element, as in Chai's case, or they have one particular skill like telekinetic magic, far sight, speed, and so on.

"A pari-pari egg, when it hatches, is raw, uncrystallised magic. The pari-pari have to guide the magic to crystallise into a pari-pari, but for a short period of time, the hatchling is unlimited pure magic, which hasn't yet been given form."

I suck in a breath. Raw, uncrystallised magic that hasn't lost any of its potency to the crystallisation process... I can't even fully grasp the implications of what it could mean for a powerful Mayak to have access to something like that. A powerful Mayak who wanted to destroy Mundanes.

"The pari-pari don't breed the same as any other creature," Ilmu continues. "They actually reproduce without any physical contact with one another. What they're effectively doing is creating more magic in the shape of an egg, and they then transform that magic into one of them. Which is why they need the connection to ancient tree spirits. There isn't enough magic in recently planted trees for them to draw upon. So you can imagine why, in the last few decades, it has become incredibly difficult for them to reproduce. Which is why the slightest rumour of a new pari-pari egg is something to pay attention to."

"And if you put that in the context of a war brewing..."

"Exactly. This is why the pari-pari have always been secretive about their eggs and their young. To ensure none of the Mayak try to take over a hatchling. Uncrystallised magic in the wrong hands could be turned into a devastatingly destructive weapon."

"I spoke to an old pari-pari who said the fate of their species depended on that egg staying safe."

"Precedence. Once a pari-pari egg has been taken over, it will happen again. The pair-pari could be forced into extinction by the Mayak in order to provide them with the weapons they want. Greed isn't solely a human trait. If young pari-pari aren't allowed to be, eventually the pari-pari will all be too old to make new eggs, and the race will die out with them. This hasn't happened so far because very few know how pari-pari eggs work, and even less know how to find pari-pari. But whoever controls that first hatchling can use it to find more pari-pari and ensure that any future eggs produced meet a similar fate. In times of peace, this wouldn't be an issue. But in times of war..."

I nod, feeling slightly dizzy at the implications of what will happen if I don't keep the egg safe. "Can you tell me about Sarroch?"

"Sarroch?"

"Yes. The one with a glamour that owns Sarroch Industries. What kind of creature is he?" I'm taking a gamble. In normal circumstances, this would be a faux pas of large enough proportions that Ilmu would be within her rights to throw me out on my ass. But we're not in normal circumstances, and I need to know what I'm up against.

"If he hasn't revealed his true form to you, it's not for me to give you his secrets."

"But you just told me about the pari-pari."

"Because they gave you their egg. They've already trusted you with their most precious possession. What I've told you are just details."

"So when you said you weren't on the Mayak's side, that only goes up to a certain point."

"I didn't say I wasn't on the Mayak's side. I said I was happy to help the Touched. But that doesn't mean I'll just betray anyone's secrets. And unless Sarroch sees fit to reveal his true form to you, I certainly won't."

"He tried to have me killed, and he tried to get the egg from me. You said you don't want the egg to fall into the wrong hands. He's the wrong hands, and I need to know what kind of being I'm up against."

Ilmu gives me a wide-eyed, unblinking look. "A powerful one."

"Wow, thanks. So helpful."

"You're welcome."

I stand up, rapidly growing annoyed. "That was sarcasm."

Ilmu nods. "The lowest form of wit. I won't hold it against you."

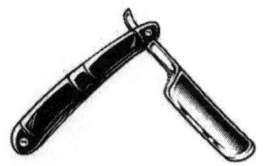

22

I leave Ilmu feeling irritated. This is the thing with the Mayak. Their logic and their traditions don't necessarily have anything to do with reason.

Once I reach my bike, my irritation has made way for worry. Now that I know the true implications of Sarroch getting the egg, I find myself itching to get back. I ride home as fast as I can. What if Sarroch came and tore my place to pieces, killed Hunter and Chai, and took the egg?

I break multiple traffic laws, but when I arrive, my door is locked, not hanging off the hinges, as it was in my imagination, and I enter to find Chai attempting to get Hunter to catch treats as he throws them. It's safe to assume Hunter will have missed every time.

"Darling, you're back. I was starting to worry. Did you get anything of use?"

I tell Chai about the pari-pari egg, the uncrystallised magic, and the potential war that's brewing while Hunter jumps all over me, completely oblivious to the fact that the world as we know it might end.

"It all makes sense," I say. "That's why the pari-pari came

to me and not Mr. Sangong. The pari-pari watched me arrive at the barbershop, and they would have seen Mr. Sangong arrive and leave. If they wanted his help, why wait for his departure? They waited until I was alone on purpose. And that's also why they were so scared, because of the risk that one of the Mayak would attack them for the egg. There was a werecat and kitsune in the shop when they arrived. I clearly don't represent the same kind of threat as a Mayak, though."

Hunter has finished his greeting.

"Whisky?" I ask Chai.

"Pudding, you read my mind."

I get to take home the almost-empty bottles from the lounge area at the barbershop, so I currently have a bit of Hibiki, which is an amazing Japanese whisky. The bottle is also worth more than two months' rent. I pour us two tumblers, both with rocks.

"So why wouldn't you be a threat?" Chai asks, taking his drink. "Because you can't use the egg? Uncrystallised magic shouldn't be restricted to the Mayak, since it's limitless."

"No, but maybe the pari-pari gambled that either I wouldn't understand what the egg represented or that if I did, I wouldn't want to turn it into a weapon that could potentially be used to wipe out humans. Let's be realistic. If I attempted to wield that kind of magic, someone more powerful would find a way to take it away from me."

Chai raises an eyebrow. "Someone like Mr. Sangong?"

I frown, and Chai raises his glass, causing the ice cubes to clink.

"Sweetie, I know you're very fond of your Mr. Sangong, but look at the facts. He found out about the egg and sent you to Sarroch so he could take it from you. That screams 'evil mastermind.'"

"That doesn't quite fit, though. I told him about the egg right away. He had plenty of time to come and take it. Why send me to Sarroch, anyway? Why not take it himself? He easily has the power to do so."

"Maybe he has a reputation to protect. Keep his good-guy image pristine."

"Why would he care about his reputation given what's at stake? And he'd only have lost his reputation with me, and I don't matter in the grand scheme of things. Look, I agree that something about Mr. Sangong's behaviour in all this doesn't add up, but I still don't think it points to him wanting to take the egg. He could have taken it last night—why let me leave with it?"

"What if he has an ulterior motive?"

"You're starting to sound paranoid."

"Paranoid sounds healthy, in light of recent events. And just because I'm paranoid doesn't mean they're not out to get me."

I snort with laughter and take a sip of the Hibiki. It's unbelievably smooth with notes of smoke and cacao—delicious. "I just don't think that 'they' include Mr. Sangong."

"We're Touched, and he's a Mayak, Api. Wake up and smell the magic. Of course he's on 'their' side."

"But the Mayak has two factions, or so Ilmu said, and one of them doesn't want war. Given that Mr. Sangong hasn't done anything to take the egg himself, that probably points to him not being in favour of going to war with humans. Which makes him one of the good guys."

"A baku told you that, though, and the baku are part of the Mayak."

"The baku also can't lie," I point out.

"Fair point. I'd forgotten about that. Okay, so I guess that probably means Mr. Sangong's legit."

"Maybe Mr. Sangong genuinely thought that Sarroch could help but made an error in judgement. He healed Hunter. He didn't take the egg... I think it's far more likely that Sarroch is the one behind it all."

Chai nods. "Agreed. So we need to work out his next move."

"And we need to understand why he bothered to make sure I survived back at the Crane."

"Did you ever find out whose blood you were fed after the mandurugo attack, by the way?"

I feel a shudder of revulsion. "No. I left immediately to look for Hunter. It would have had to be some kind of vampiric creature, though." I drink some more whisky, suddenly feeling the need to wash away the imaginary taste of blood in my mouth. "Do you know what? We're over-thinking this. I'm just going to book a flight to go back to my parents' place and, from there, find the pari-pari's relatives. It's what they wanted anyway, and that will keep the egg away from those who want to get their hands on it."

"What of the supernatural set in England? Would they know about the value of a pari-pari egg?"

"One thing at a time, Chai." I pull out my phone and start looking at flights.

"Hold on. You're not the only who had the idea of booking a flight."

I look up at Chai. He shows me his phone. He's pulled up the site of Panong's airport. Apparently due to a technical failure, it's closed for a few days, and all flights are grounded. "You're kidding. You think the Mayak did that?"

"Sarroch's the head of a very large company, so he'd probably have the technological resources to achieve something like that. Or it got done using magic. Some magic fries technology."

I rub a hand on my face. "What about boats? I could try to get on a cargo ship bound for Vietnam."

"You could, but that would mean crossing the whole island to get to Penghan Harbour. Not something to do at night, given the way things are."

"And Sarroch works in shipping." I shake my head. "What the hell was Mr. Sangong thinking, sending me to him? He's made a proper dog's dinner of this."

For a while, we drink in silence. I get up. "I'm going to put some music on. The silence feels oppressive." I pick Ella Fitzgerald. We need some girl power.

Then I remember something. "You know, when the pari-pari couple entered the barbershop, neither the werecat nor the kitsune seemed to sense the egg, or they'd have had some sort of reaction. The egg is too much of a big-news item for them to not care. In fact, the pari-pari couple would have had to pass near a few Mayak between the forest and the barbershop, and yet no one did anything? On top of which, the mandurugo asked me for the egg as if they thought I had it with me. They couldn't tell it wasn't in my bag."

"You mean you think that the egg can't be sensed."

"Must be. Maybe it has its own kind of magical defence. Can you sense it right now?"

"No, but that doesn't mean much, since it's not metal. Even you are better at sensing than me, and that's saying something."

"Thanks, Chai. Way to make a girl feel good when she's down."

Chai gives me an impish grin before turning serious again. "It does, however, explain why Sarroch needs you alive and functioning. If he can't find the egg by himself, he needs you to give him the egg's location."

"Exactly."

"That's probably his move—keep track of you until you lead him to the egg. He didn't attack when you were at the barbershop because it's Mr. Sangong's territory. Mr. Sangong helped bring you home last night as well, so he couldn't attack you on the journey over."

"And Mr. Sangong set up some security on my house as well. That might be why he didn't try something today."

Before I can add anything more, there's a knock at the door.

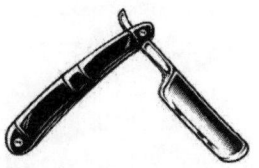

23

Hunter starts barking. Chai and I exchange a look.

In the time it takes me to stand up, Chai has drawn all my cutlery to him, and it's rapidly reshaping itself into various weapons. Like I said, Chai's the kind of guy I'm always glad to have at my back.

I head to the door and glance through the peephole. "It's Mr. Sangong."

Chai nods but doesn't relax. The cutlery returns to its natural shape, but I notice he leaves the knives within close range.

I open the door.

"Apiya. How are you doing?" Mr. Sangong steps inside.

Hunter hurries over to greet him. Surely the fact that Hunter likes him is confirmation that I'm right about him being a good guy.

"I see Hunter is back to normal. I wanted to come check on you. And there's also much we need to discuss."

"We do," Chai says acidly. "Like why you thought it was a good idea to send Api to Sarroch."

Mr. Sangong gives him a slight frown. "Sarroch is... I've

known him a long time. Centuries. He's a decent person. But with everything that's at stake at the moment, his views might have diverged from mine without me realising. It's been a little while since I've spent proper time with him." With Mr. Sangong that could mean a few months or a couple decades.

"You mean about the war?" I ask.

"Ah, you've found out." Mr. Sangong sighs. "Yes, about the war."

"What's your stance on it?" Chai asks.

"Would I have a Touched for my protégée if I were in favour of culling humans?"

"Sending her to the Crane without backup to meet with someone who might want to kill her in order to get the egg doesn't strike me as the behaviour of someone looking out for a protégée," Chai replies coldly.

Mr. Sangong bows his head. "In light of last night's events, I recognise that I probably made the wrong decision there. I had assumed Sarroch would help, but I may have been mistaken."

"*May*?" Chai asks acidly. "Anyway, why even leave Api to deal with the egg? Why not take care of it yourself? Given the context and the potential war brewing, she's not exactly equipped to deal with it, is she? No offence, sweetie, but you're hardly the toughest Touched on the block."

"Thanks for the vote of confidence."

"Because the pari-pari gave her the egg," Mr. Sangong replies. "I respect and trust their decision. If they chose her, it was for a reason."

"Is Sarroch pro-war, then?" I ask.

"Sarroch hasn't picked a side either way. It's part of why I thought he'd be a good option to help with the egg. He's continuously refused to declare himself for one side or the other. He's normally quite balanced in his opinions and careful in making decisions."

"What happens if he gets the egg?"

Mr. Sangong pauses. "Magic works in many ways like nature—everything is in balance. The very powerful Mayak with enormous life spans breed with great difficulty to ensure that they don't take over everything. Every Mayak has a weakness, and for each weakness, there is a being who can take advantage of that. This creates an equilibrium. Every Mayak has a predator. It ensures no one can go on a rampage and destroy everything. There will always be a Mayak who can stop even the most terrifyingly powerful beings. But if someone corrupts a pari-pari egg... raw, uncrystallised magic has no weaknesses. It has nothing to slow it, to keep it from taking over. It would, in essence, be like an invasive species that has no predators. That means that once a pari-pari egg has been corrupted, it cannot be undone. It cannot be stopped. The world will fall into chaos."

"And the pari-pari gave *me* their egg?" It wouldn't be exaggerating to say that I'm feeling a tad overwhelmed right now.

"Yes, why didn't they keep it?" Chai asks. "Surely they are the most suited to protecting it, as they have always done."

"Something must have changed. Something that made them believe they could no longer keep the egg safe."

"But what—"

"Apiya, since you're safe, we will discuss all this later. For now, I need to attend a Mustering of Elders. As you can imagine, there have been many Musterings of late."

"Wait, you're leaving?" I wouldn't like to admit it, but I'm feeling a hell of a lot safer with Mr. Sangong around.

I also finally understand why he's been so distracted and

absent from the barbershop of late—probably attending Musterings.

"You'll be safe so long as you stay here. The Elders and I will deal with Sarroch in due course."

"And the mandurugo?" I glance out the window, where twilight is rapidly approaching. Mandurugo can operate during the day, but they're much more powerful at night. The thought makes me shudder.

"The mandurugo are not smart enough to act of their own initiative on this. They are simply responding to their master's orders." Mr. Sangong heads to the door.

"Wait. What if I give you the egg?"

He stops, looking startled. "Why would you do that?"

"To keep it safe."

He hesitates, as if torn. He sighs and shakes his head. "You cannot. You were chosen, Apiya, and you must bear the responsibility that you were given. And it wouldn't be wise anyway. The temptation would be too great, even for one such as I. I will help you by going to the Elders, but until then, you have to be the one to keep the egg safe."

I nod. Handing off the egg would have been far too easy. "Can you sense where it is right now? The egg?"

Mr. Sangong smiles. "Clever girl. Yes, that is the egg's natural defences—I cannot sense it, nor can any other Mayak. So only its caretaker knows where it is. Now I need to go. Stay here—I'll send word."

Once he's gone, Chai picks up the whisky bottle. "Top up? I guess we might as well make ourselves comfortable since our plan for the night is to stay here and sit tight."

"Thanks for staying."

Chai rolls his eyes. "Like I'd walk out and leave you on your own at a time like this. That would make me a pretty shitty friend, wouldn't it?"

Before I can answer, my phone rings. "Hello?"

"Apiya?" The voice is deep, smooth, familiar. "It's Sarroch. Where can we meet? I need to talk to you."

I'm gripping the phone so hard, my hand aches. "Sarroch? You want to meet?" My voice is faint.

Chai is gesturing at me manically.

"Yes, I need to see you."

"Er, what... why?" I'm having a hard time thinking straight.

Chai starts to type furiously on his phone, then he shoves his screen in my face. *Hang up. He could have powers through voice contact.*

"We need to talk about what happened last night," Sarroch says. "About the egg. I assume you've recovered?"

I feel an odd sensation, a sensation I've felt before, as if I'm falling. "I..." My blood seems to have turned to milk. My mind feels all warm and confused, like I'm about to fall asleep.

Chai clicks his fingers in front of my face, jabbing his index finger at the message on his phone. I know he's right, but for some reason, I can't bring myself to hang up. In my mind's eyes, I see a huge pair of dark eyes, and gold flickers in their depths, beautiful and hypnotic.

"Where can I come to see you?" Sarroch asks in a low voice.

Chai makes a grab for the phone. Reflexes kick in, and I dodge out of his grasp, but the movement is enough to jolt me back to myself.

"Barbershop," I blurt. "I'll meet you at the barbershop." I hang up before he can say anything more.

"What was that?" Chai asks.

"I don't know," I reply shakily. "I just... I couldn't hang up. But then when I ducked away from you, it was like that feeling let go of me for just a second. Enough to hang up."

"The bastard was manipulating you over the phone."

"I think so." I take a deep breath.

"You okay?"

"I'm fine. Annoyed, a little rattled, but fine."

I dial Mr. Sangong's number, but it goes straight to voice mail. "Great, no help there."

"Well, we just let Sarroch go to the barbershop. He finds no one there—"

"And then what? Calls me back and gets me to do something like invite him to my house?"

"If he calls, you just don't pick up."

"What if he can force me to pick up from a distance?"

"Can he do that?"

"I don't know! I don't even know what being he is. I have no idea what his powers or his limitations are. But he's obviously got some abilities at a distance. And the baku confirmed that he's powerful, so we can't afford to underestimate him. I say we go to the barbershop—"

"No way. That's as dumb as a girl wearing a tiny dress in a horror film going to investigate a suspicious noise in the night. You're not pretty enough to die stupidly, darling."

"Another incredibly backhanded compliment. Thank you. But let me finish. If we don't go, Sarroch is likely to keep looking for me, because I'm the only lead to the egg. You heard what Mr Sangong said—the egg can't be sensed. Which means that as long as I don't get caught, staying away from it is the safest thing I can do for it."

"That makes sense, I suppose," Chai says grudgingly.

"Mr. Sangong has a security spell in place at the shop, and I'm keyed to it. Sarroch enters the barbershop. We catch him in the spell, and he's trapped until Mr. Sangong returns. That way he can't make it to my place."

"What if the spell isn't powerful enough to contain Sarroch?"

"It's designed to be able to contain any Mayak, in case I'm alone and in trouble. Plus Mr. Sangong will know that something's going on at the barbershop, so he can come back."

"I still don't like it. He told us to stay here."

"Well, I like the idea of Sarroch trying to break into my place even less, so I'm going."

"Fine. Fine. I'll come with you."

Hunter whines when he sees me grab my jacket. I kiss his velvet head and stroke his ears. I don't like the idea of leaving him behind so soon, but so long as Sarroch is looking for me, being near me is probably more dangerous for him than being on his own. "I'll be right back. Mr. Sangong said I'd be safe here, so you'll be safe here too. Don't worry." The latter I say more to myself than to him.

I glance at the courtyard. No one knows where the egg is except me, so it should be safe too—so long as no one catches me and forces me to reveal its location.

24

Chai insists that we drive over to the barbershop even though it means we'll have to leave the car parked illegally.

"Darling, I think we have more important things to worry about than parking tickets right now."

"Fair point."

It's a five-minute drive, but I have to admit I'm grateful for the protection of the car. Now that night is rapidly falling, the shadows clotting the narrow streets of Old Town suddenly look sinister.

Old Town streets have a very distinctive layout. The buildings' upper storeys jut out, so they overhang above the pavement. This provides shelter from the rain, which is heavy in the wet season, and it means that at night, unless there are lights by the front doors, all the building entrances are hidden completely in the gloom.

In short, it's perfect for creatures of the night to hide in and stalk prey from.

I realise I'm chewing my fingernails.

"We're in a car made of metal," Chai says calmly, as if reading my thoughts. "No one can attack me in here. This is *my* domain." He gives me a quick wink. "I may be a fairy, darling, but this fairy's got claws."

I snort with laughter.

He parks in front of the barbershop, and we quickly check that the coast is clear before rushing from the car and straight into the shop.

Tim is sleeping in the lounge area, and he looks up as we enter. "Your dedication to your job is impressive, treacle." He stretches. "I wasn't expecting you to come in today. In fact, I was very much expecting to take the day off, so don't expect me to work. I'm getting ready for a marathon nap session." He yawns.

"That's what you do every evening. But listen, Chai and I are here because we need help."

"Why does that sound like trouble?"

"Sarroch is coming here, and we're going to trap him in Mr. Sangong's security spell."

Tim jumps up to his feet. "Are you barmy? What you gonna do that for?"

"Because he's tried to kill me once already, and now he's trying to find me, probably to do it again. He's after the egg, Tim, and I can't get ahold of Mr. Sangong since he went to an Elder Mustering. So unless you can get him to come here and deal with Sarroch, we're on our own."

"It's impossible to communicate with anyone taking part in a Mustering. No one can interrupt or interfere with the Elders when they gather. No magic can get through."

I thought as much. "Well then, there you go. So it's just us, and Sarroch is on his way. Unless you fancy your chances going up against him?"

Tim stretches again and gives me a haughty look. "I fancy my chances going up against anyone, sunshine. I'm not running scared of some geezer, no matter if he's Mayak. But as it stands, it's not worth my while, and I don't feel like it, anyway."

"What a coincidence."

"Hmm, yes."

"Look, I just need to know whether the security spell will be enough to contain a being as powerful as Sarroch."

Tim hops to the floor. "It should be. It was designed to be, but that was a few decades ago..." He crosses the barbershop.

"Where are you off to?"

"Going for a walk."

"Now?"

"Yep. Important cat meeting to attend. Felines only. You know how it is..."

"You coward! You're just going to leave Chai and me to face Sarroch alone?"

"I'd help, I really would, but I can't miss this. Highly important cat business and all. Cheerio!" He slips into the office, his tail curled in the air.

"Tosser!" I call after him.

"Trollop!" he calls back.

I turn back to Chai. "I guess we're on our own."

"You're going to have to give me a refresher on British insults. We didn't learn 'trollop' at my boarding school."

"Sure thing. As soon as we've dealt with the small matter of a powerful Mayak coming our way, it's top of the list."

I head to the wall next to the entrance. There's the stone I can imbue with messages, and next to it, embedded in the wall, is a Lei Ting curse charm. It's a large copper disc the size of my head with a square hole in the middle. Ancient protection symbols are embossed on its surface. The charm is keyed to me, so I can activate it.

I place my hand on it. The metal is oddly warm to the touch, as if it has been held in a giant palm all this time.

"It's weird. I can see it's metal, but my magic isn't picking up on it," Chai says.

"Maybe because it's a charm, it can't act like normal metal?"

I feel a shiver run through me from the contact with the disc followed by the licking-battery-feeling of magic. I can activate the charm without touching it, but it's trickier, and I don't want to risk anything going wrong.

The activation complete, I can feel the dull pulsing of the protection charm on the air, like a heartbeat. "Can you sense that?"

Chai frowns. "What?"

The charm is supposed to be undetectable to anyone other than those it's keyed to. I used to activate it anytime I came to work, but I never had any troubles, and over the last couple of years I stopped bothering.

My phone rings. "It's Sarroch," I hiss.

Chai tenses visibly as I answer.

"I'm outside," Sarroch says.

This time I don't feel that falling sensation. He's not trying to control me.

"Well, I'm inside. Come on in."

"No, I think you should come out here."

"Why?"

"I'd rather not be in Mr Sangong's space." He hangs up.

I look at Chai in panic. "He wants me to come outside."

"Don't do that."

"Thanks, Captain Obvious. Any other pearls of wisdom?"

Chai runs a hand through his hair. It's the first time I've seen him unsure. "Do you think he knows about the security spell?"

"Maybe. It's supposed to be a secret, but who knows."I bite my lip. "I know. How about I call back and tell him the egg is in here, and that I don't feel safe bringing it out in the open."

Chai nods. "Okay, that might work."

I call Sarroch.

"What?" he snaps before I can speak. "I said *come out here*. Right. Now."

I blink as an odd feeling comes over me again, and it's not until Chai yanks the phone from me and hangs it up that I realise I was already walking to the barbershop's entrance.

"So that didn't work," Chai says.

"I guess my only option is to get out there in person and tell him about the egg being in here."

"Remember my previous point about stupid girls dying in horror movies?"

"What other option is there?"

"We wait in here."

"No. He might have ways of finding out where I live. While we hide in here, he could go there on his own. I'm not putting Hunter in danger again. We need Sarroch to enter the barbershop and get caught by the security spell, and if I have to go out myself to make that happen, then so be it."

"Okay. But if anything goes wrong, he's getting crushed by my car."

"Yes please."

My palms are sweating. I don't even know if Chai can do

that to a Mayak. Sarroch might be too strong to get crushed. Too fast. He might be able to move objects and have more power than Chai. He might have a strong affinity to metal. The possibilities for things to go wrong are pretty endless.

"Here goes."

25

I step outside the barbershop. Sarroch is leaning against Chai's car bonnet. He's wearing jeans and a black V-neck jumper. As soon as he sees me, he straightens up.

"Whose car is this?" His eyes lock onto mine.

"Ch-Chai..." I whisper, my mouth dry as sandpaper buried in a sand dune.

Sarroch takes a step towards me, frowning. His eyes are black, and I start to feel the falling sensation. My breath flutters in my chest.

"Is Chai a threat? What being is he?"

"Just a Touched."

"Good." He takes another step, eyes boring into mine. "Take me to the egg. Now."

"I..."

"It's for the best, Apiya. I must have the egg. Give it to me."

The falling sensation intensifies. "It's inside," I manage to squeak while I'm still in control of myself.

The falling sensation fades a little. "Inside the

barbershop?"

I swallow. "I'm too scared to bring it outside."

Sarroch frowns.

"I feel safe at the barbershop," I add.

"I see. I suppose that makes sense."

Still, I sense hesitation from him. He doesn't want to enter the barbershop for some reason.

"Where is Sangong?"

"He's at a Mustering of Elders."

Sarroch frowns, his eyes glazing over. Then he nods once to himself, apparently satisfied. Did he just check Mr. Sangong's location? Or about the Mustering?

"Okay. Let's go, then." He takes my arm in his death grip and marches me toward the barbershop's metal shutter.

I lift the shutter, and we both slip underneath it, passing through the illusion to the barbershop. Sarroch's hand at my triceps feels like a claw—he's practically cutting off circulation. He must be able to feel the frantic rhythm of my pulse.

He stops me from going any further, keeping me at his side as he scans the barbershop. "Is that Chai?"

I nod. Chai sits on one of the chairs of the lounge area, looking the embodiment of the nervous little Touched. If there's one thing he's good at, it's looking like he'd be a wet blanket in a fight.

Can Sarroch sense the trap? I can feel its pulsing around us, but Sarroch shouldn't sense it any more than Chai could.

I can't trigger it, though, not while I'm in contact with Sarroch, or I'll be trapped in it with him.

"I'll go get the egg," I croak.

"Yes."

Sarroch relaxes his grip, and I remove my arm, careful not to appear too eager.

"Api, now!"

I dive to the side.

With a flick of his wrist, Chai has the iron shutter wrap itself around Sarroch. Sarroch reacts so fast it's as if he knew what Chai would do before he did it.

The shutter never touches him. Instead, it melts away, turning into molten liquid. But the distraction is enough for me to get far enough from Sarroch. I trigger the trap.

Whomp. It's like all the air got sucked out of the room for a second.

My gaze meets Sarroch's. I've never seen such murderous rage directed at me before. Sarroch's mouth opens as if he's yelling, but the trap swallows sound to stop anyone from using any voice-based magic.

He opens his hands. *Whomp.* The sound is so deep it echoes in my chest like the base beat at a nightclub. Something invisible between Sarroch and I ripples.

"Shit, he's attacking the trap!" I yell.

"Time to go." Chai grabs me.

We run for the entrance. The shutter has gone, but the illusion will keep the Mundanes from seeing the barbershop for now.

Another *whomp.*

We stumble out into the street. "How long do you think we have?" Chai asks.

"No idea."

He waves a hand, and the shutter of the next shop moves to rearrange itself at the barbershop's entrance. "We need to make sure we're not around if he gets out before Mr. Sangong gets back."

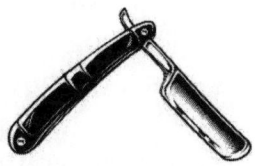

26

"You grab Hunter and the egg, and you come back to my studio," Chai orders as he drives us back. "At least until we hear from Mr. Sangong. There might be some security in place on your house, but I doubt it's powerful enough to stop Sarroch, and I defend myself best when I'm in my own territory."

"What about Fergie and the rest of my critters?"

"I doubt Sarroch is fussed about them. Hunter, though, might attack him if he breaks into your place, so it's best if he stays with us."

He brings the car screeching to a halt outside my building, and I jump out the door. I burst into my house, pushing past Hunter as he comes to greet me.

The egg is still in the hutch, but as I pull it out from the false bottom, my heart sinks. "Shit, shit, shit, shit!"

"What?" Chai is keeping an eye out at the front door.

"The bloody egg has started hatching! Look, there's a crack down the top of the shell there. And a tiny piece of shell is missing."

Painfully bright blue light streams out of it like a beacon, as if wanting to notify every magical creature within the city.

"What the hell do we do with it?"

Mr. Sangong's words about the consequences of an egg being corrupted ring in my mind. "We can't keep it here. What if I corrupt it by accident? I have no idea what's supposed to happen once it's finished hatching. I need to get it to the pari-pari. They'll know what to do." I curse. "Why is it hatching so soon?"

"How are you going to find the pari-pari, though?"

I squeeze my eyes shut in frustration. "I should have taken the extractor—I have the tears of the two pari-pari parents. I could have summoned them." The extractor is still tucked away in the safe at the barbershop's office. Obviously, there's absolutely no way to go back and get it now, not unless I want to experience firsthand whatever Sarroch's doing to the barrier.

"Okay. Okay. You said you saw a pari-pari at the forest by the Crane, right? By the river?"

"Yes. Yes! Let's do that. We'll take my bike, though—I'm not risking getting stuck in traffic, and a car is easier to ambush."

I grab my keys and my helmet and throw Chai the spare helmet I keep for friends. The egg I wrap into a towel and slip it into my satchel. The egg's light thankfully seems to be swallowed by the towel or the bag. Either that, or the egg somehow understands it needs to stay hidden.

Then Chai and I head out. I feel a brief spike of worry for Hunter, but it's definitely better for him to stay here for now.

It seems almost laughable to lock my front door, as if that would stop a Mayak truly determined to get in. I push away another spike of worry. Hunter will be fine, and he can't get out to come after me with the door locked.

We step out of my building into the street.

"Why is it that we keep meeting when you're trying to get your motorbike?" a woman asks.

The four mandurugo step out of the shadows. They surround Chai and me.

"Whoever helped you keep your place of living hidden did a thorough job," Red says. "But in the end it wasn't enough." She smiles wolfishly.

"And this time we're doing it right," Slick Back says.

The Mandurugo rush us. They're fast, but so is Chai. His car spontaneously disassembles, sheets of metal slamming into them.

The mandurugo stumble, surprised.

Slick Back recovers first, leaping towards Chai, his face a snarl. The car's bonnet flies at him. He's forced to dodge.

Red rushes towards us but gets attacked by sharp bits of metal that create a cutting tornado around her. The car's engine flies at Shorty, and he has to jump back to avoid being crushed.

The bumper wraps itself around Black, pinning her arms to her sides as she screams with rage.

Chai laughs. "Is that the best you got?"

Like I said before—Chai is a badass when it comes to a fight.

Slick Back dodges a large piece of metal and would have reached Chai if not for the car's bonnet sliding between them just in time. The bonnet reshapes itself to scoop Slick Back and toss him a few metres back.

"Api, take your bike and go."

"What? No! I'm not leaving you."

"I can hold them."

"I'm not—"

My motorbike slides towards me in a screech as the kick-stand scrapes against the ground, raising sparks.

"Go!" Chai shouts. "We can't risk you getting caught. I promise you I can hold them."

I watch him for a moment, slim and handsome, surrounded by a maelstrom of twisted metal. The mandurugo barely seem to notice me, all their attention focused on him.

He's right. If I get caught, the consequences don't bear thinking about, and as shitty as it feels to leave my friend behind, I'm not going to get a better opportunity to get away from the mandurugo.

I swing my leg over my motorbike, then rev it to life.

The mandurugo screech, finally noticing me. Mr. Sangong was right. They aren't very bright. Two of them lunge after me, but a pair of car doors catch them, twisting around them. They manage to slip away, but they're forced back in front of Chai.

He doesn't look at me. "Go!"

With a final glance at him, I ride off, my engine roaring into the night.

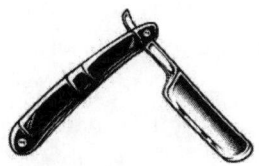

I make it to the Crane without trouble and leap off my bike. I throw my helmet aside, not bothering to chain it or the bike, and I run into the forest.

The night has fully settled now, the darkness beneath the trees as deep as squid ink, the air full of the singing of insects. Branches snap beneath my boots, and I feel as discreet as an elephant trundling through the bush.

At least hopefully it means the old pari-pari by the river will know I'm coming. I rush through the vegetation until I reach the stream. "Hello?"

I step into the stream, the water running over the leather of my boots in case it helps. "Hello! I need to speak with you."

The forest remains empty. "I spoke to you last night. I need your help—please."

Still nothing.

"It's about the egg."

Silence.

I hope I'm not doing something incredibly stupid, but I don't know what else to do—I gently pull the egg from my satchel and unwrap it. Whereas before the towel seemed to absorb the light, now the egg is shining so brightly that the towel almost seems to be absorbed.

"You have to help me with the hatchling. I don't want to corrupt it. Please come and take the egg to guide it properly."

Still nothing. I'm starting to feel afraid now. Seriously afraid. Anybody coming in or out of the Crane is going to see the light and come for me. Or even worse, what if it's already too late to stop the hatchling from becoming corrupted?

"It's your egg!" I yell. "Why the hell won't you come and claim it?"

And then I hear a sound that chills me all the way to my spine's marrow. A rustling nearby, and the soft cry of a baby.

A pontianak.

I remember Yue yesterday and how beautiful she was. Pontianaks feed on humans to maintain their beauty, and they have an incredibly creepy hunting method. They imitate the crying of a baby that's been abandoned to lure humans in.

Again I hear a rustling and a baby crying. It's coming from behind me, so it's between me and my motorbike.

I don't hesitate and spring forward into the forest. There's no point being quiet—she knows I'm here.

I shove the egg back into my satchel, but it's no longer enough to swallow the light. Blinding-blue shards shoot out from every gap in the satchel, piercing the darkness, alerting everyone to my presence.

The light is so bright it blinds me, robbing me of any night vision. My progress is slow and clumsy—I stumble over every last twig. My breathing whistles loudly in my ears.

I don't notice a branch across my path, and I tangle my feet in it. I go sprawling into the leaf litter, earning myself a face full of dirt. The impact sends a painful jarring up my wrists.

In the quiet, I hear an even worse sound. The crying of a baby again, but this time further away. If I wasn't already sure I was being stalked by a pontianak, that would be the confirmation. Pontianak hunt by confusing their prey—the further away the cry of the baby, the closer the pontianak is.

I scramble to my feet and spring forward. Branches target my clothing, scratch at my hands and face. Some of the scabs on my face reopen, stinging. Trickles of blood run down my cheek.

A soft baby's cry comes from my right, so I plough to the left, not caring what direction I'm running in.

"Someone help me!" I yell. "I need the pari-pari! I call on the pari-pari!" I have no idea if there are words to summon them. "I call forth the help of the pari-pari! As the egg's caretaker, I request assistance!" I shout every semi-formal-sounding phrase I can think of, but nothing helps.

They're probably hiding from Yue.

The baby cries are barely audible now. She's catching up with me. And somehow, she's now to my left.

I throw myself to the right. Have I gotten turned around in my mad race? I have no idea.

I let out a cry of fear as I hear the tiniest baby's gurgle so soft and close, it feels like a baby just whispered into my right ear. I can't help myself and look back over my right shoulder. The darkness is thick, impenetrable.

Maybe if I'd been looking forward I'd have seen it, but looking over my shoulder, I had no chance.

The ground disappears from under my feet, and I'm

tumbling downwards, ass over head. I land on something hard, making a strangled noise as the air leaves my lungs.

Wheezing and a little dazed, I push myself back up as quick as I can and into a defensive stance.

"I really don't understand why the pari-pari chose such a weakling to care for their egg."

I've fallen into a natural clearing, and Yue is arriving from the other side of it.

"You wouldn't believe the number of times I have hunted by scaring my prey into running and falling into this very clearing." She laughs. "Humans are so predictable. You cannot resist reacting to the cry of a baby, whether to run towards it or be so terrified of it you completely lose the ability to think properly."

There are fewer trees here, and between the egg and the moonlight, it's almost bright as daylight, if daylight were a world of muted greys. The black leather Yue's wearing gleams in the light, as does her shiny black hair arranged in artful waves. The deep V in the opening of her skintight jacket shows a slash of mother-of-pearl-pale skin. Her eyes have turned red, shining brightly in the dark.

Yue comes towards me, with the grace and confidence of a predator sure of making its kill. "I'm impressed that you managed to get away from my mandurugo a second time. But in the end, a weakling like you will never be a match for the likes of me—not even with Sangong granting you protection and hiding your home. Now. Give me the egg."

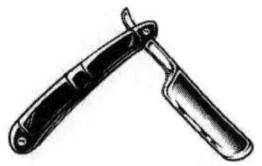

28

I pull the egg out of my bag. The light intensifies, creating a mad gleam in Yue's blood-filled eyes. The light is so strong I can see the bones through the skin of my hands. I can't see any details on the egg anymore, but I can feel cracked shell and a hole with my fingers.

"Yes," she hisses. "Give it to me."

I know I can't use the egg and all its magic to stop her or save myself. If I do that, I corrupt it, with all the consequences that follow. If I do that, Yue wins by default because I will have turned it into corrupted magic she can use. The egg is designed to be a pari-pari. It has to become a pari-pari.

I can try to fight Yue off and hope that, by some miracle, I'm strong enough to take on a pontianak. Except I know that I'm not. Pontianaks are the most powerful of all the vampiric species. The queens of the vampires.

Yue reaches for the egg. Her hand is so pale it seems to merge with the light.

If only I knew the egg better, I might be able to suggest it follow the nature it was meant for and become a pari-pari.

I've barely spent any time with it, and it normally takes me at least a full day with an object before my magic will work.

But the eggs knows me. It knows my rabbits and Hunter. It knows my little house, my courtyard, my bag. And I remember what the old pari-pari said—all that matters is someone taking care of it, not how they do it.

All I can do is try, because I'm out of all other options.

I reach out with my senses for the egg with all the power and focus I can muster and do my best to nudge it, to suggest that it should become a pari-pari. I bring up its parents in my mind's eye, to help guide it. I bring up the feelings of peace, of trees, of the quiet places at the back of a cave I had from them. And I feel something shift within the egg. Something like a release.

Yue's hands land on top of mine, grabbing for the egg. Her sharp nails slice my skin. A stench of rotting corpses mixed with frangipani flowers rolls off her.

"What are you doing?" she hisses.

I feel the same growing heat, the constriction at my throat I felt back at the Crane when Yue attacked me. I don't try to block it. Instead, I encourage the egg, feeling like I'm gently coaxing a child.

"No!" Yue rips the egg from me. The nails on one of her hands rake against my ribs and down until they slice deeply into the side of my waist.

I stumble but keep my focus, managing to keep my connection to the egg. I can barely breathe, needing to expend massive effort to suck in a tiny bit of air, and each breath causes a massive flare of pain at my waist.

But I can sense a faint satisfaction to it, a feeling of things neatly falling into place, the way they were meant to be. After all, I'm not encouraging it to go against its nature, but to follow what it was created for.

Yue screeches in anger. She's holding the egg in front of her face, although it's no longer visible among the searing light.

I keep on coaxing, gently suggesting, bringing up every image, every reference I have to the pari-pari.

"Stop that!" Yue throws the egg aside and launches herself at me. "Stop it!" Her face is twisted with rage, her nails reaching for me.

Pontianaks normally eat their victims' hearts first. I've heard what they can do with their nails, and given the wound at my side, I know the stories aren't exaggerated. I close my eyes, wincing and bracing for the impact.

A low roar tears through the air like a plane passing too low overhead, so deep and so loud it makes the ground shudder. I open my eyes.

Yue's on the ground to my right. And standing in front of her is Sarroch.

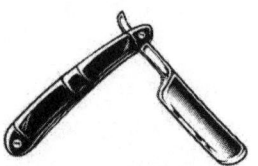

29

"What are you doing?" Yue snarls, getting up.

"Enough," he replies calmly.

"She ruined the egg. That filthy little maggot did something to it."

"You can't accuse her of ruining it, given that it is following what it was meant for."

I sit up in spite of the searing pain in my side. I bring my hand down to it, which is a mistake because I feel the size of the wound gaping open. For a heartbeat, I think I'm going to faint, but I manage to cling to consciousness.

Over where Yue dropped the egg, there is now a small creature. It still glows but nowhere near as bright as before. Its skin is pale yellow, almost the colour of straw, and its hair stands out from its head exactly like straw. It's looking down at its tiny hands in fascination.

"You're a traitor." Yue jabs a finger at Sarroch. "And I will see you punished for it. Now stand aside. I'm hungry." As she says the final words, her gaze falls on me.

She steps towards me, but Sarroch puts an arm out. He shakes his head slightly. Something happens between them, something I can't see but can just about feel. It's like a vibration, like tension given physical form.

For the briefest moment, Yue's face shifts. It's like getting a peek behind the façade, the beauty fading away, and I get a glimpse of something yellowed and wrinkled.

Yue steps back abruptly, and the vibration stops. There's fear in her eyes, and then her expression settles into a sneer. "I will ruin you for this." Then she turns around and marches away. She disappears into the gloom much faster than she should have, as if she summoned the darkness to swallow her.

Sarroch turns to me.

"You stay the hell away from me," I warn, although my order would probably sound a lot more impressive if I weren't bleeding and struggling to get up to my knees.

"I just saved your life."

"Only because the egg was no longer of any use to you."

"That may be, but I could have left you to Yue. Now let me help you up. You need to be seen to."

I shake my head, and through sheer stubbornness, manage to get myself up on my feet.

A bad idea. The world sways dangerously then goes dark.

I'm starting to make a habit of this.

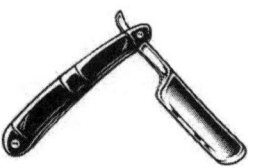

30

I come to once or twice, but other than confused, blurry impressions, I don't see much before I pass out again.

By the time I come to properly, I'm back in my bed. I stir slowly, reaching down to the wound at my waist, but it's covered with a bandage.

"Easy, petal," Chai says in a low voice, coming to my side.

"...happened?" A croak would be a generous word to describe the creaky sound that comes out of my mouth.

Hunter's hearing has obviously gone supersonic because he begins to whine and scratch at my bedroom door.

"We can't have him in here jumping all over you—it could reopen the wound. But he's been very worried about you, and with reason."

"How long...?"

"Three days. Mr. Sangong kept you unconscious. You'd lost quite a lot of blood, and pontianak claws are apparently poisonous, so we've been having to fight quite a bad infection. Mr. Sangong thought it best for you to sleep and let your body rest, and I agreed with him."

Chai gives me a glass of water with a steel straw sticking out of it. The straw shifts and reshapes itself until it finds my mouth. I gulp cool water down, throwing Chai a grateful look.

Chai returns the glass to my bedside table and sits on the bed, next to my legs. "I'm guessing you want to hear what happened?"

I nod.

"Although I'm never one to underplay my abilities, four mandurugo to deal with was getting a bit tricky for me. They were getting faster and better at anticipating my tricks. They made me sweat, sweet pea. Can you believe that?" Chai laughs, flicking a strand of hair from his forehead. I know him well enough to realise that this is a euphemism for "I very nearly died."

"Your Mr. Sangong arrived just in time. I wasn't best pleased when he showed up with Sarroch in tow, though. But they took care of the mandurugo, then they wanted to know where you'd gone. I wasn't going to tell them, but somehow, I found myself saying that the egg had started to hatch and that you'd gone to the forest to give it to the pari-pari. Mr. Sangong actually paled, and Sarroch said the word "Yue." I didn't know what that meant at the time, but I've since found out."

"Not a word you want to get familiar with."

"I don't know what Sarroch did, but there was a really loud roar, like a jet passing too low overhead. It actually made the ground shake. Then he was gone. From what I understand, you know what happened after that..."

Chai falls quiet, and in the silence, Hunter's whining grows louder.

"Can you please let him in?" I ask. "You can hold him

back so he doesn't jump all over me. It doesn't seem fair to leave him out there."

Chai grins. "I thought you'd ask that, so I came up with a solution."

He opens the door, and Hunter leaps in. He stops abruptly, and begins walking in an odd, stilted fashion. As if something else is operating his legs.

Confused, he looks over at Chai, who laughs.

"I put metallic bands on each of his paws so I can control his movements."

In his odd, halting way, Hunter makes it to the bed and climbs up. He starts to whimper and whine, his tail and his body wiggling with excitement as he gets closer to me.

"Shhh, Hunter, shhh." I stroke his head and his ears. It makes me feel a hell of a lot better. And that's about all I remember until the next time I wake up.

———

THIS TIME I HAVE MR. SANGONG AT MY BEDSIDE. "WELCOME back, Apiya." He also gives me a drink of water, although without a magically extending straw. "How are you feeling?"

"Like a pontianak sliced me open. How am I healing?"

"Very well."

I frown. "Mr. Sangong, why didn't you just heal me the way you did Hunter?"

"We'll discuss that later. For now there are more pressing matters to attend to."

"Like why you freed Sarroch from the barbershop?"

"Sarroch is not above making mistakes, no matter the number of centuries behind him. But he wasn't seeking the egg to corrupt it. He wanted to get it from you because he thought you were a danger to it, and he wanted it under proper care. Unfortunately, since he has a rather poor opinion of the Touched, rather than attempting to explain that, he just tried to manipulate you and force you to give it up. Old creatures can be like that. We are sometimes unable to see the straightforward path because we still operate as if we were living in a previous century. Yue, on the other hand, was very much after the egg to corrupt it. She is the reason the pari-pari gave it up in the first place because she started to hunt them to get their egg."

"Where is it now? The little—was it a pari-pari, what the egg turned into?"

Mr. Sangong nods. "I'll help you."

Even with his help, it's difficult to get out of the bed. The movement tugs at the wound at my side, making me gasp in pain.

"Here, you can lean on me like this."

Mr. Sangong helps me to the living room and from there to the kitchen. There seems to be something going on in my courtyard. All my creatures are gathered around one of the rabbit hutches, apart from Fergie, who is stuck behind the trellis again.

Inside it, almost blending in, is the baby pari-pari.

"It seems to have taken the rabbit hutch as its home environment," Mr. Sangong says.

"Is that even possible? I thought pari-pari needed trees and nature..."

"There's a lot we still don't know about magic and how it operates and changes and evolves. We might be witnessing the next step in pari-pari evolution."

Mr. Sangong brings me back inside, and we sit on the sofa.

"There's something else," I say. "Hunter came to me all

the way at the Crane, when neither you nor Chai heard my call for help. What's that about?"

"We'll discuss this later."

"At the same time as we discuss why you didn't heal me like you did Hunter?"

"Exactly. There will soon be a Great Mustering, and given recent events, you will have to attend."

"A Great Mustering? What's that?"

"A Mustering is just the Elders gathering. A Great Mustering is when all the Mayak gather."

"And you want me to come? I'm not suicidal."

"This is the first time a Touched has been so deeply involved in our affairs. Your actions with the egg put an end to plans that were made by some Mayak, and there has to be a reckoning."

I gulp at the mention of a reckoning. "Hold on. I saved the egg, and as a pari-pari, the egg is Mayak. So I saved a Mayak. And there's plenty of Mayak who didn't want a war and, therefore, who wouldn't have wanted Yue to get the egg, right? Why does there need to be a reckoning?"

"Because there are also plenty of Mayak who are very much in favour of war. They're the ones demanding a reckoning. Don't worry, though. I'll be right there with you the whole time. You'll be fine."

Funnily enough, that does very little to reassure me.

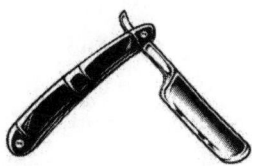

31

Although Mr. Sangong doesn't heal me like he did Hunter, he has me drink some horribly bitter concoction a few times a day that speeds things up so that, by the time of the Great Mustering, I'm able to walk without pain, and the scratches on my face are barely visible. I'm still in no shape to spar, but at least I can get around without help.

Luyang Temple is on the top of a hill, in a clearing. Panong is such a hilly, volcanic island that construction can only happen on the edges, leaving the centre mostly untouched. The hills are normally covered with dense vegetation, the kind of forest I was in with Yue a few days ago.

This particular hill, however, although as densely covered as the rest, has an empty spot on its crown. It isn't man-made, and nature has never encroached on it for some reason. Well, the reason probably has something to do with the amount of magic gathered there.

Luyang Temple is believed to have been built in the tenth century. It's our biggest and oldest temple, and it's always busy with people coming to pray and make offerings.

But in the dead of night, it's empty, and Mr. Sangong and I are alone as we approach.

In front of the temple is a flagstone courtyard, and directly opposite to the temple's entrance is a massive two-sided drum laid out in a frame on its side about half a metre from the ground.

On either side are two huge cast-iron braziers. Chunks of perfumed wood or incense burn in the braziers along with the coal, so the smoke that rises is fragrant.

As we get near, the smoke from the braziers takes shape and coils over towards the drum. The smoke begins to move rhythmically, and a deep thumping rings out from the drum in response.

The smoke has no shape to it, no head and certainly no eyes, and yet I can feel a twin set of gazes on me as we pass the drum, much like with the smoke creature at the Crane.

The beat of the drum is like hearing an enormous heart-beat, measuring out the seconds as Mr. Sangong and I cross what feels like the endless expanse of the courtyard. I can hear our footsteps in between each of the heartbeats, but otherwise the night is perfectly silent.

Near the temple are two rows of cast-iron pots, hedging the arrival path. The pots contain sand, holding the joss sticks that worshippers stick in each day. Some are tiny, skinny things, some much fatter, with large glowing embers. Only a few are still lit, the rest reduced to sad, stumpy skeletons.

The temple ahead is a large square building with the traditional three-tiered roofs with the corners that curl up at the ends. The tiles are jade, the supportive beams, buttresses, and columns all painted a bright, gleaming red that currently looks grey in the moonlight.

An enormous set of doors block the entrance. Two door

guardians are painted on their surfaces. The doors are tall, equivalent to almost a storey and a half of a regular building.

I've never been here at night, and something about the doors and their guardians look forbidding—I suppose that's the point.

The two door guardians step out of the wood, growing into three-dimensional creatures. They're as big as the doors themselves, dressed in intricate armour of gold and sapphire and emerald. One door guardian's skin is red, while the other's is blue. Both of them have long beards and moustaches that reach their chests, and they both hold beautiful but enormous ceremonial jian swords, the blades made of rippling, folded steel. Chai would be impressed.

They stand in front of the temple's entrance, and they don't look particularly disposed to letting us in.

"Maybe they won't let us pass," I say hopefully.

Much as my curiosity is most definitely piqued, my survival instinct is even more triggered. Something tells me that going beyond those doors is not the option you take when a long and healthy life is your priority.

"Let me talk," Mr. Sangong whispers. "In fact, it would be best if you stayed completely silent until this whole thing is over." He looks up at the two door guardians. "I bring, as is my right, a guest, one who has been Touched by magic."

"And who is the one who comes before us today?" the red-skinned door guardian asks in a booming voice.

His tone makes it sound like this is an exchange of ritual phrases rather than an actual questioning.

"I am—" Mr. Sangong makes a long string of sounds that no human tongue could replicate. "Sangong" is obviously some kind of shortened nickname for us common mortals to use. I wonder if they're speaking Panongian for my benefit.

"You may enter."

The two door guardians step aside, and the enormous wooden doors open of their own volition. The temples doors don't reach the ground. Instead they are held within a wide wooden frame, which means the threshold is barred by a thick beam of wood, about twenty centimetres or so.

Beyond it I can see the regular temple, where the Mundanes go to pray and make offerings. There's the front hall, which leads to an internal courtyard that's decorated with statues. Then beyond is the main hall, where the altar and shrine will be. The temple is perfectly dark and quiet.

The beam of wood across the threshold is believed to keep evil spirits at bay, and it's considered to be extremely bad luck to step on it.

And with good reason.

Mr. Sangong and I walk up to the threshold, then we both step up onto the beam. We have to pause for a second to allow the slow shifting of realities. And then we step down from the beam and into the Mayak's temple.

As with all the spaces inhabited by the Mayak, the temple is far greater than the temple in the Mundane reality. Enormous coils of incense hang from the ceiling, turning slowly like enormous corkscrews and spreading their spicy, woody-smelling smoke. But unlike Mundane incense, the burning embers don't progress up the coil, so there is no ash dropping on the floor. Instead the incense coils burn on indefinitely, never changing.

I'm not going to lie, I most definitely approve of this. Cleaning up crumbled ash is a pain in anyone's ass.

Stretching ahead of Mr. Sangong and I is a wide passage lined by stone columns. The columns are black and painted with gold symbols, but they're neither Panongian nor Chinese. I'm not even sure my father would be able to identify them.

Hanging at each column are beautiful palace style lanterns with fine but intricate wooden frames, across which stretch painted silk panels. Red silk tassels hang from each lantern corner. But looking up at the lanterns above the entrance, I see neither lightbulb nor candle within. Instead, the lanterns themselves give off the light.

Beyond the lanterns, the ceiling looks like the roof of a cavern, all rough grey stone. I can only see the stone at the edge of the temple, right above the entrance. The rest is swallowed up by darkness.

But that's not what's caught my attention. Thousands and thousands of delicate, glittering beads that look like glass hang from the stone on threads of gleaming silk. Glowing blue lights are scattered throughout the beads, like so many stars in the sky. I have no idea what this is, what the beads are for, or what causes the blue lights to shine.

Then I see something move within the darkness above the lights. Something fat and undulating. I quickly look down. Whatever it is, it's not the kind of creature whose attention I want to attract.

Mr. Sangong touches my shoulder, no doubt to remind me to stop gawking like a tourist. That's not going to win me any points with the Mayak.

I realise he has already taken off his shoes, and I quickly remove my boots, hoping I haven't already made a faux pas by not doing it immediately.

We start walking down the aisle. The stone beneath my feet is strangely warm, as if heated. On either side of the columns, two large crowds have gathered. The Mayak watch Mr. Sangong and me, and the looks are not all friendly. I recognise quite a lot of faces from the barbershop, and some people nod or smile in acknowledgement while others wear hostile expressions.

Some have chosen to wear their human glamours. Some shifters are in their human form, while others are in their true forms. It feels like walking through a pantheon of every myth and story I've ever read about. Everyone is dressed elegantly, some in modern day suits and dresses, others in beautiful traditional dress.

I spot one of the female mandurugo wearing a shimmering gold Singkil type dress and veil, very similar to the traditional Filipino dress. There are beautiful kimonos, semi-transparent kebaya, brightly patterned batik sarongs.

I look more out of place than ever, though, in my ripped fishnets, torn denims, and leather jacket, but it's better this way. Any attempt to fit in would have smacked of desperation because *everyone* present knows I'm just a Touched and therefore don't belong.

Mr. Sangong and I continue our progression down the aisle, our footsteps loud in the charged silence. The air is thick with magic, and I can feel it buzzing against my skin. It's quite an overwhelming thing to be in the presence of so many supernatural creatures and having all of them directing their attention onto me. I swallow, feeling a tightness in my chest.

In fact, if Mr. Sangong weren't at my side, I would be sorely tempted to turn around and run away. My earlier impression was correct—this is not the best place for my health and longevity. Some of the looks I'm getting are reminiscent of what a gazelle must experience when a pride of lionesses is nearby. I have no particular wish to share the gazelles' experiences.

"You'll be fine," Mr. Sangong whispers. "Just let me handle everything."

"Come," a deep voice rumbles. The voice rattles in my skull, in my rib cage, in my whole body, compelling me forward.

The row of columns ends in a wide space, where normally the shrine and the altar would be. My palms begin to sweat at the sight of what is waiting for us there. An enormous seven-headed snake towers three metres high, the rest of its enormous body curled up in a huge coil, making it hard to judge just how big it is when fully stretched out. Twenty metres? Thirty? Its scales are iridescent, shimmering between turquoise and cobalt, with a black ridge along the spine. Its belly, heads, and the tip of its tail, are all bright red.

Mucalinda. The nagaraja—the king of the naga. The naga are single headed serpent-like creatures with a lot of water-related magic.

"I didn't think he was real," I whisper.

"*She*," Mr Sangong murmurs in reply.

"Oh, I didn't realise. She's always referred to as male in Mundane legends." Dad will be besides himself with excitement when I tell him that Mucalinda is female.

Mucalinda is such an old creature and is so close to uncrystallised magic that she doesn't ever take human form, nor does she come to the world of the Mundanes, instead solely existing in spaces like this one. She made a single, notable exception, coming to protect the Buddha from the rain—the Buddha being sometimes referred to as the only enlightened Mundane the world has known. I never thought I'd ever see Mucalinda in person. To me, she still feels like a mythological creature, separate from all the other Mayak.

"I present Apiya Chapman, Touched by magic and my protégée," Mr. Sangong says with a bow.

I match his bow, wondering if I should curtsy. But a curtsy in biker leathers would only look ridiculous, and I really don't want to risk offending Mucalinda.

"And I accuse Apiya Chapman of conspiring to bring about the destruction of the Mayak," a woman calls. A woman whose voice I recognise and who I would have preferred never to see again.

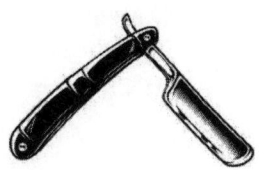

32

Yue is as beautiful as ever. Her glossy black hair is pinned up in an elaborate arrangement full of red and gold combs. She wears a blood red hanfu dress, the wide sleeves and waist trimmed with cloth of gold, embroidered with tiny red flowers. Her skin is as flawless and glowing as mother-of-pearl. And yet her beauty is less intoxicating now that I've had a look behind the façade, now that I've had that glimpse of withered, sallow skin.

She steps up to stand on the other side of me from Mr. Sangong. "We have been struggling with the matter of Mayak survival in the face of the Mundanes' gradual destruction of the world. I had found a way to guarantee our safety and stop the Mundanes, a weapon that would have ensured we won once the war begins. The raw, uncrystallised magic of a pari-pari hatchling. But Apiya Chapman interfered and took the egg for herself, either for her own ends or to ensure the Mayak's downfall." Yue spits my name, her black eyes as venomous as a coral snake.

I open my mouth to protest, but Mr. Sangong's hand squeezes my elbow.

"Apiya did not use the egg for her own ends. Nor did she seek the Mayak's downfall. Rather she encouraged the egg to fulfil its intended purpose—to become a pari-pari. She helped ensure the natural order of things was maintained."

"The natural order of things currently involves the Mayak barrelling towards extinction. Apiya's action sought to maintain that, which is as good as threatening us. By the Ancient Rules, anyone or anything threatening the Mayak must be destroyed. So Apiya Chapman must cease to exist for the same reason that we have to go to war with the Mundanes."

Okay, I'm sweating freely now. I don't have a snowball's chance in hell if Mucalinda agrees with Yue's version of the facts.

"Apiya prevented the corruption of the egg belonging to one of our most ancient and treasured creatures. She ensured a new generation of pari-pari was made. She *saved* a Mayak. She didn't threaten or destroy."

"On top of which, I was asked—"

"The Touched will be quiet, or I will silence it!" Mucalinda thunders. Her voice is as deep and loud as the cracking of mountains.

I realise I've hunched over by reflex, my hands over my ears. I straighten up slowly, more than a little frightened.

"You see," Yue says, turning to the assembly. "No respect for her betters. The Touched think of themselves as *equal* to the Mayak. They have no regard for magic, even though it has chosen to smile on them."

Hostile grumbling spreads through the crowd. Mr. Sangong gives me a pronounced stare. Yep, I'm aware I just made things worse for myself. I will most definitely stay quiet now. I hadn't realised his warning not to say anything had to be obeyed to the letter.

"Yet the Touched are human!" Yue points an accusing finger at me. "Virtually the same as the Mundanes, who are currently threatening our existence."

More grumbling.

"We all know how difficult it has been for the pari-pari to make eggs of late," Yue continues, "which again is caused by the Mundanes' destruction. And now that we lost this one opportunity that would guarantee we could win the war against the Mundanes, it might be decades before another pari-pari egg is made and we have such a chance again."

A kitsune in true form steps forward. "And what is a decade to the Patient Ones? I hope, Yue, that you are not embarrassing yourself and displaying the heart of a child within these hallowed walls."

I recognise Ari's voice, one of my regulars at the barber-shop. His true form is like a large red fox, with deep russet fur and black tips to his ears as well as his paws. He's beauti-ful, which I expected, given how charming he is in human form. I smile gratefully at him, and he gives me a wink. He has a lot of tails, more than ten—even older than I'd guessed.

"A decade is but the blink of an eye to us Patient Ones," Yue replied coldly, "but it is not so for the Mundanes. They run around so quickly, changing so fast, that ten years for them is a lot of time—time enough to do enormous damage. We have underestimated their ability for destruction and how much of it they can achieve in their short, pitiful lives. If we wait another ten years without doing anything, how much more will be lost? Imagine if one day they decide to destroy this temple to build one of their beloved shopping malls or some apartment block?"

The crowd mutters and shifts uneasily.

"Let's be reasonable," Mr. Sangong says. "One thing the

Mundanes are very passionate about is their religions. This temple is a monument to their religion, and they're hardly likely to tear it down. This is important to them."

Yue smiles triumphantly. "To the older generation, yes. But young Mundanes don't come here. Or very few of them do. Their worship takes place on the internet and in shopping malls. In ten years, those young Mundanes will be making decisions that could have a devastating impact on us all." She turns to the crowd, spreading her arms, her long sleeves framing her body. "This is why we must go to war *now*. We are fortunate in Panong that the destruction has been slow, but mark my words, we will gradually follow the fate of places like Singapore, where almost all the Mayak have been forced to flee. If we do nothing, Panong will one day become a sterile desert. We must fight back. We must stop the Mundanes. And we must also make an example of any Touched who interfere with our plans, or they, too, could become a threat to our survival."

The crowd shouts its approval, staring at me. Not a friendly face in sight. I suddenly feel very small, very powerless, and very, very mortal.

"Mr. Sangong?" I whisper.

33

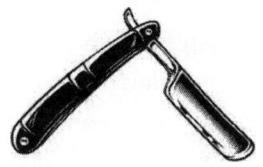

Out of the corner of my eye, I see a small creature step forward.

"The pari-pari have an announcement to make," a female voice says.

The crowd instantly falls quiet, the shouts replaced by whispers and murmurs as everyone shifts, trying to get a better look.

The pari-pari has skin of a deep chocolate brown threaded with glowing copper swirls. Her eyes are slitted like a snake's and emerald-green flecked with gold. Her clothes—if they can be called that—seem to be made of iridescent turquoise and cobalt scales that match Mucalinda's. She also has the same scales covering her hands, feet, and parts of her forearms and shins, like gloves and boots. Her wings are the same brown and copper as the rest of her but thin and a little rumpled, like those of a butterfly recently emerged from a cocoon.

Compared to most of the creatures present, she looks tiny, almost insignificant. There is no sense of power to her, of danger, there is nothing awe-inspiring. Instead, I sense earth and damp, dark, quiet places where time flows slowly and where creatures move in careful, halting steps.

And yet the respect the Mayak give her is undeniable.

"As of today, the pari-pari are divorcing from the Mayak." She speaks in a low voice so everyone has to remain deathly quiet to hear her.

I can see people straining to hear. The silence is such, you could have heard ash break if the incense coils weren't magical. Shock ripples through the crowd.

"Our most precious possession, one of our eggs, was hunted by a Mayak. As you all know, this has happened before—even the Mayak are not immune to greed. But in the past, others have always taken steps to stop the hunt before anyone got close to our eggs. Where were Yue's predators this time? The magic, in its wisdom, gave each of us a predator so no one creature could be above the others, but greed and fear has so infected the Mayak that no one stood up or did anything as Yue stalked and hunted us for weeks in order to find our egg. We are the most defenceless of the Mayak, so any person present here today could have helped us, even if their powers weren't enough to stop Yue. It would still have been more than what we could do by ourselves."

The pari-pari speaks calmly, almost gently, but all eyes are suddenly looking away in shame.

"Our situation was so dire that we had no choice but to ask a Touched to help us," she continues in a voice that's barely more than a whisper, "knowing that a Touched wouldn't want our egg to be corrupted. A *Mayak* had to go to a *Touched* for help!" Her voice is suddenly as loud as a granite boulder cracking, like a smaller version of Mucalinda. She might have claimed the pari-pari are defenceless, and she might have no power I can sense, but there is the same strength to her voice as there was in Mucalinda's.

"The Elders should have protected us. The Mayak should have protected us. You all failed. You are no longer worthy of having the pari-pari among your ranks. Effective immediately, we are striking off as an independent entity. We no longer consider ourselves subject to any ties or alliances with the Mayak. We have no responsibilities to the Mayak, and we owe you no loyalty. Let it be known that if you declare a war, the pari-pari will side with the Touched. So the queen of the pari-pari has spoken."

She bows low to Mucalinda and walks out, trailed by consternated silence. For a couple of heartbeats, no one speaks. Then shouting and arguments erupt all over the temple.

"Silence!" Mucalinda booms.

The noise is snatched away along with my breath. It literally feels like a hand reached into my lungs and seized my air. Not as painful as getting winded by a fall but still unsettling. I take a deep breath.

"Yue, your response to this?" Mucalinda asks.

She shrugs her slender shoulders. "Sometimes sacrifices have to be made for the greater good. The survival of all the Mayak is at stake. The pari-pari would have made other eggs. If the war had been successful, they would have had more forest to make more eggs from, so they would have thrived with the rest of us. The outcome was worth the sacrifice."

"Sangong?"

"I disagree. These are sacrifices we cannot afford. If we prey on each other, we have no chance of surviving the Mundanes. We must be united to have strength, and we *must* ensure that we care for the weaker amongst us. What is the point of winning against the Mundanes if, to do that, we sacrifice the very thing we are attempting to save? We have lost the pari-pari. What else will we lose if we follow Yue's course? How many other Mayak will have to be sacrificed for the cause?"

I can feel the crowd's energy change. They've been rattled by the pari-pari, all right, and they seem far more receptive to Mr. Sangong than earlier.

"And whose place is it to decide which beings are worth sacrificing and which are not? Would Yue agree to sacrifice herself for this cause she's espousing?"

Yue narrows her eyes. But before she can reply, someone else steps out of the crowd.

"I agree." Sarroch. He's wearing a perfectly tailored light grey three-piece suit. His hair is swept back, and he's sporting neat stubble on his jaw, which suits him better than the clean-shaven, businessman look.

"I accuse—" Yue again makes a long string of sounds that starts with something vaguely like "Sarroch" then becomes incomparable to human sounds. "Of conspiring with the Touched to bring about the Mayak's downfall."

"Enough, Yue," Sarroch says.

She glares at him defiantly.

"I helped stop you from corrupting the pari-pari egg. If I am guilty of anything, it is of that which our pari-pari queen accused us all. It is to my greatest shame that while I took action, I took it far too late. As Sangong just said, nothing is worth sacrificing our own, not even defeating the Mundanes. I still refuse to declare myself for or against war. I believe that having two factions weakens us—look at what it has led to today. But I will declare myself against anything or anyone seeking to destroy or corrupt another Mayak in service of their goals, whatever that goal might be."

"That goal is to ensure the Mayak survive," Yue says haughtily.

"Let us discuss this," Mucalinda says slowly. "The survival of the Mayak. While I do not approve of sacrificing our own, I do not see anyone else suggesting a way out of our current predicament."

"Actually, I would like to propose a solution," Mr. Sangong says. "A solution to our problem with the Mundanes that doesn't require war and doesn't require the corruption of magic. As you all know, I have been in favour of attempting to infiltrate Mundane society and change it from within in a way that helps us." He places a hand on my shoulder. "Apiya has been my protégée for eight years, and she has been working with me for five."

I look over at him, feeling very, very weary. Changing Mundane society is just a *little bit* of an enormous, over-whelming, *impossible* task. Even Mundanes struggle to change their own society.

"A great many of you are already familiar with her and her skills with a razor," Mr. Sangong continues. "Her magic is a peculiar kind of home magic that cannot be used to harm. She cannot, therefore, directly hurt us."

"She could—" Yue begins then does an odd gasp.

"Your time to talk has ended, Yue," Mucalinda interrupts. She has snatched the breath from Yue as she did to us all just moments ago.

"Apiya knows the Mundane world," Mr. Sangong continues, "the world of the Touched, and she knows the Mayak through her work at my barbershop. She grew up in Europe and yet is Panongian. She is one who straddles multiple worlds. That is what we need. A bridge. Something to make the link between ourselves and the Mundanes, that we can find a way to continue to coexist peacefully."

"And how will she achieve that exactly?" Yue asks.

An excellent question, to which I have no answer because I cannot believe that Mr. Sangong is putting me forward for this. How the hell am I qualified to ensure Mundanes and Mayak coexist, given that I'm neither? And obviously I can't say anything because speaking up is likely to only make things worse for me. Turning down the job is also likely to rapidly decrease my life expectancy.

"The pari-pari chose her to care for their egg," Mr. Sangong continues, as if Yue hasn't spoken. "That is an extremely auspicious sign. We all know that in spite of having very little in the way of physical powers, the pari-pari are closest to raw magic than any of us. They are moved by creation itself. If they chose Apiya to help them, I say we follow their wisdom and see what Apiya can do to help secure our place in this modern Mundane world."

"And you believe she can do this?" Mucalinda rumbles.

Who can blame his lack of confidence?

"I do, yes."

The seven serpent heads look at me. I do my best to look confident and capable and not like a scared little Touched with the most useless magic of all.

"I refuse to leave the fate of the Mayak to a Touched," Yue spits.

"Rather than argue this, why don't we agree to a trial period?" Sarroch says in a conciliatory tone. "A year is nothing for Mayak and Mundanes alike, but it's enough time to know whether this experiment works."

Yue opens her mouth to reply, but Mucalinda rumbles. "Hmmm. That is true. A year. Very well. Apiya Chapman has a year to deliver the coexistence of the Mayak and the Mundanes."

Which is *such* a small ask...

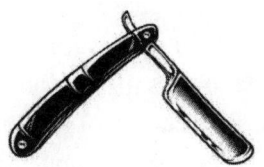

34

As soon as Mr. Sangong and I are back in the safety of the Mundane world, under the normal stars, I whirl on him. "What the bloody hell was that? How the hell am I supposed to deliver something like that? What the hell is going to happen when I don't deliver, which I won't? I didn't sign up for a slow and painful death at Yue's hands!"

"You'll be fine, Apiya."

"I will not be fine if I fail. And I will fail. I have no idea how—"

"Don't go exhibiting the heart of a child," Mr. Sangong reproaches calmly. "You don't need to know all the answers right at this moment."

"No, just within a year."

"Which is plenty of time."

"No, it's not. It's nothing in terms of time. You of all people should know that."

"Then we'd better start work soon," Mr. Sangong replies mildly.

"Why did you do it?"

"What?"

"All of it. You must have known about Yue stalking the egg."

"I heard rumours..."

"So why leave me to deal with it?"

"Because the pari-pari chose you, and I meant what I said back at the temple. Their wisdom is like the wisdom of magic, and we should always try to listen to it as much as we can. As to putting you in charge of finding a solution to our problem, if I hadn't done something like that, you would have been destroyed, Apiya. The Mayak do not take well to the Touched meddling in our affairs."

"I didn't meddle. I was dragged into it by the pari-pari and left in that mess of a situation by you."

"The Mayak were unlikely to see it that way. Look at how they reacted to Yue's arguments. This way everyone is happy. You're safe, and I get to push through the solution that I wanted, namely to find a way to infiltrate the mundane world and get them to change their behaviours."

"Everyone is happy apart from me."

"You're still alive..."

"For now."

"Pessimism doesn't suit you, Apiya. You should go home. Get some rest. I will leave you a few days to recover, then we have much work to get on with."

"Wait. The pari-pari queen said no one helped even though you all knew about Yue hunting the egg. Why didn't you help?"

Mr. Sangong doesn't reply. His eyes glitter in the moonlight.

"If you knew Yue was hunting the egg, you knew I was in

danger the moment the pari-pari came to me. Why didn't you warn me? Why send me to Sarroch instead?"

"We'll discuss this later, Apiya."

"Right. When? When we talk about why Hunter was able to come to me during my fight with the mandurugo and why you didn't heal me like you did him?"

Mr. Sangong smiles. "Exactly. Now get some rest." He pats my shoulder then walks off into the dark, disappearing as if the night has opened its maw and swallowed him whole. The Mayak are disturbingly good at doing that.

Muttering to myself, I walk over to my bike, put my helmet on, and kick the old girl to life.

* * *

The moment I enter my house, both Chai and Hunter jump on me with equal enthusiasm.

"What was the temple like?"

"I need a drink."

"Well ahead of you, sweetie. I have gin martinis ready to go."

For once I don't protest. It's the middle of the night anyway, and I really do need a stiff drink. I finish saying hello to Hunter and give him his traditional well-done-for-staying-on-his-own treat. It bounces off his nose, as it always does, and I help him find it. Then Chai and I get settled on the sofa with Hunter lying against me, his head on my thigh.

"So come on, darling, I'm on tenterhooks. Spill."

I tell Chai about the whole experience. When I get to the part about the pari-pari announcement, Chai gasps. When I tell him about Mr. Sangong's suggestion as to my role going forward within the Mayak, his jaw looks like it's in danger of detaching itself from the rest of his head.

"I know. And Mr. Sangong is acting like none of this is a big deal. I'm freaking out at him, telling him that I'm totally unable to deliver on what he's promised, and all he tells me is not to be impatient, then pats my shoulder and buggers off into the night."

"For your mentor, Mr. Sangong doesn't seem that preoccupied about your health and ability to stay alive."

"I know. All this time he's been so over-protective, telling me all about how the Mayak are too dangerous for me, and now he drops me right in the deep end. It will be bad enough trying to survive the next year, but when we get to the end of the year and I've not delivered what he's promised, I can't imagine Mucalinda will say, 'Good job. You did your best, and that's what matters.'" I take a big gulp of the martini. The alcohol burns a trail down my throat and into my stomach.

"So, what are you going to do?"

"Not a bloody clue. Hope that I somehow manage to pull something out of my ass that allows me to stay alive."

"Hmmm. Well at least this promises to be an entertaining few months."

"Thanks. I'm so glad my impending doom counts as entertainment for you."

Chai grins. "What are friends for? In any case, you won't be doing this on your own. I'll be right there with you."

I smile back. "Thanks. And I've got Hunter as well." I stroke the top of his head and his silken ears. "Chai, we never discussed what happened that night—the night he came to me."

"I have no idea. We were outside. I was taking him for a walk, and all of a sudden, he goes tearing off, ripping the leash out of my hands. He disappeared before I could catch up with him."

"Did you hear anything? Did you sense something?"

Chai shakes his head. "Nothing. Maybe you and Hunter have a bond that's different from what the rest of us have. You know, since you have that weird thing of getting acquainted with objects before your magic can work with them."

"That's true... it would also explain why Hunter feels so important. When he was hurt, before, it felt like I might lose a part of myself. But then, I should be able to call Hunter like that all the time, and I don't feel anything different right now."

"Did you ask Mr. Sangong about it?"

"Yeah, but he keeps fobbing me off, telling me that we'll talk about it later. I'm trying real hard not to have the heart of a child, but it's pretty damn difficult when I've got no answers and more questions than I can shake a stick at."

"His change in attitude towards you is real weird too, going from 'the world of the Mayak is too dangerous' to leaving you in charge of the egg, given the situation."

"Exactly. Apparently, a lot of people knew about Yue stalking the pari-pari, about the egg, about the potential war. Mr. Sangong must have known, and yet he acted like it was no big deal for me to take care of the egg. Why?"

"He must have some kind of ulterior motive."

"I tried to ask him about that, too, but he wants to talk about it later."

"Apiya, I know you care for and respect Mr. Sangong," Chai says carefully, "but how well do you actually know him?"

"I... I thought I knew him well. We used to work together a lot at first, at the barbershop. Lately he's been more distant, but until recently I'd have said I knew him very well. Now, I don't know... I'm not so sure."

"We should be careful, Apiya, and not trust him too completely. He might have a hidden agenda that he's using you for."

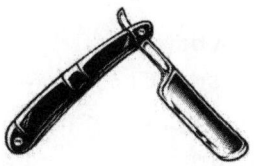

35

My phone beeps, and I check it—a message from my mother asking that I call them as soon as I can.

"Just a sec," I tell Chai. I call Mum. "Hey, motherload, everything okay?"

"She's on the phone!" Mum calls. "One moment, darling. Your father has something to tell you."

I hear grumbling in the background. Dad doesn't want to come to the phone.

"No, it's your mistake," Mum says forcefully. "You *are* telling her about it."

"Fine." Dad comes on the phone. "Apiya?"

"Hey, Dad. What's up?"

"A very nice young man called me, asking me questions about you."

I feel a spike of worry. I don't know any nice young men. "Who? What did he ask?"

"Er, I've already forgotten his name. But he wanted to know what sort of things you liked."

"What sort of things I like?"

"Yes, you know—films, music, hobbies, that sort of thing."

What the hell? What kind of creep have I got on my back this time?

"I assumed it was your boyfriend trying to organise some kind of surprise or something like that," my dad continues.

"Dad, I don't have a boyfriend."

"Well, I just figured this Chai fellow you seem to spend a lot of time with... you talk about him a lot, and you seem fond of him, so I assumed..."

"Chai is gay, Dad," I say dryly. "I'm lacking a rather essential piece of equipment for him and me to be able to date."

"Ha! Told you," Mum says in the background.

"All right, all right," Dad says grumpily. "Well, I'm sorry. I assumed it was your boyfriend, so I was quite happy to answer all his questions."

"And you don't remember his name or anything else about him?"

Dad answers in the negative.

"What did you tell him, exactly?"

"Nothing particularly nefarious. That you like jazz and traditional Panongian opera, I gave him your favourite films, books that you like—that sort of thing. It really did seem innocuous at the time."

I can't be too mad at my dad. At the end of the day, he doesn't know what's going on here. More probing fails to reveal anything of use, so I hang up. I bring Chai up to date. Something dodgy's going on, although what is anyone's guess. It has to be Mayak related—the timing is far too coincidental. But *why* does a Mayak want to know these things?

Before we can discuss it any further, there's a knock at

the door, which sends Hunter into a fit of barking.

"How many dodgy things *are* going to happen tonight?" I mutter, climbing down from the sofa.

"This is the time the Mayak operate at," Chai says, joining me. All my cutlery is hovering defensively around us.

I check the peephole. "Looks like a delivery boy." I look at Chai questioningly.

He nods. The knives hover around the door.

I open the door, and indeed, it is a package for me. Not a regular package, given that the delivery boy has eyes like a cat's. But he doesn't do anything funny other than just give me the box and leave.

"Hold up," Chai says. "There could be something dangerous inside. Let me."

We put the box by the kitchen sink and step back to the living room. Chai is used to manipulating metallic objects from a distance, so two knives cut the box, forks and spatulas prying the cardboard open.

No explosions, no noxious gases...

Chai doesn't stop there, though. He gets a mirror to hover above the box so we can see its contents.

"What is that?" I ask as I catch sight of something gleaming and winking in the light.

"It looks like glass."

We approach the box cautiously. I gasp. Inside is possibly one of the most beautiful things I've ever beheld. It's a heart that's been shaped out of glass but not using any techniques I've seen Mundanes use. Instead of having facets on the outside, the surface of it is perfectly smooth, but the inside is a mass of tiny facets that refract the light and send sprays of rainbow light colours in all directions.

"There's a card," Chai says.

I open it. Written in very neat and precise handwriting is one line.

My deepest apologies for having a heart of glass. - Sarroch

That's another Mayak concept in the same vein as having the heart of a child. Having a heart of glass means being too quick to take offence, too quick to get upset, or being unable to tolerate someone whose views are different from your own.

"That's a pretty classy apology..." I murmur, still looking at the play of the light through the glass heart.

That will be Sarroch apologising for the way he dealt with me and with the egg. I would not have expected that from a powerful Mayak.

Another knock at the door. Another delivery boy, this one with a much larger box. Inside it is a gorgeous pakay, the Panongian traditional dress.

The top half of a pakay is tight-fitting, the sleeves flaring out from the elbow until they reach the knees. The neck opening closes diagonally towards the armpit, similarly to a cheongsam. The dress then skims the body until thigh level, where it opens, revealing the second layer beneath. The outer layer flares out at this point, spreading into a wide train.

Both the flare of the sleeves and of the skirt are composed of several layers of fabric, and the pakay is designed to be worn with the hands clasped so that the combination of the trailing sleeves and the flaring skirt create an impression of a waterfall.

The fabric itself is breathtaking. The outer garment is made of silk that has been hand-painted in an intricate pattern of cherry blossoms over a light grey background. The grey stops it all from being too saccharine. The pink of the little flowers perfectly matches the colour of my hair.

The under skirt is a pale cream that's infused with the slightest touch of pink.

There's another card with the dress.

Tomorrow night, eight o'clock, Menari Water Opera. I will send a car to pick you up.

Same neat handwriting as on the apology card.

I look up at Chai. "Well, I guess that takes care of the mystery of who called my dad."

I pull out my phone and call Sarroch. "Did you speak to my father?"

"Don't be ridiculous."

"I spoke to him. I know you asked him about what kind of music I like and all that kind of thing." It feels slightly weird to think of my dad referring to Sarroch as a "nice young man," though.

"I didn't call your father. I had one of my assistants do it. And yes, I had him enquire as to what kind of music you enjoy. I was very pleasantly surprised to hear about your tastes in water opera."

"Why are you doing this?"

"It's a little pointless to deliver an apology if the token in question is not something the person will appreciate."

"You already sent a card and the heart. Which is very beautiful, by the way. But as far as a token of apology, that's really enough. There's no need for the pakay or the opera."

"The heart is not a token of apology. That's a bit like saying the paper a card is printed on is a token of apology."

"That heart's a *little* more than plain paper, though." Understatement of the century.

"Barely," Sarroch replies negligently. "Your father said you can rarely afford to go to the opera."

"Yes, but..."

"He also said that you are saving up to buy yourself a

proper, traditional, handmade pakay."

"I am, but..."

"Excellent. Don't worry about the pakay fitting you—it's made by a Mayak."

"Sarroch, while all the information you found out about me is correct, and while I do appreciate the gesture, I really don't see why we need to go to the opera together."

"We're going to be working closely on this issue of the conflict between Mayak and Mundanes, so I think it's important we get to know each other better."

"Working closely? Together? Since when?"

"Do you really think I'll be leaving something so important to some powerless Touched? No matter that you have Mr. Sangong's approval, you are utterly inadequate for the job."

Something we agree on.

"If we are going to work together we need to be able to get along," he continues. "I'll see you tomorrow."

The line goes dead. I look at Chai, and he grins.

"Are you going on a date with Sarroch?"

"A date implies that I gave my agreement to go. I feel like I'm being frog-marched into spending an evening with him."

"I don't know, contacting your family to know what you like, sending you beautiful gifts, expensive clothes, taking you out for a lavish night out at the opera—I would imagine he has a private box..."

I roll my eyes. "Not helpful, Chai."

"Well, if your new assignment amongst the Mayak means you get expensive clothing and taken out to the opera, it's really not so bad."

"Somehow, I doubt very much that this is going to be in any way indicative of my new position within the Mayak."

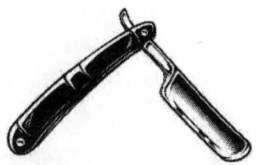

36

The following night, as he promised, Sarroch sends a car. And as he promised, the pakay fits me perfectly. Not wanting to be adorned only in things he has given me, I made some purchases of my own. I'll be eating instant noodles for the next couple of weeks as a result.

My hair is too short to be able to do anything with it, not in the traditional style anyway, so I've had to buy hair extensions then get them dyed to match my own hair. With them, I can create the complicated knots which make up the traditional hairstyle worn by Panongian women.

Hair ornaments made of mother-of-pearl and red glass nestle within the intricate loops. The coloured hair combs and my hair perfectly match my new pakay.

Much as I'm not particularly looking forward to an evening with Sarroch, I have to admit I feel like a princess. And I can't believe that I get my very own traditional pakay, and a hand-painted one as well—I shudder to think how much that's worth these days.

When Sarroch said he was sending a car around, I

assumed it would be one of those slick black affairs with tinted windows—although hopefully not something as crass as a limo. I think there are only a handful of limos in operation in Panong, and anyone riding in one just looks like they're making a desperate plea for attention.

Instead, I'm greeted by a midnight-blue 1960s Isuzu 117 Coupé. It's a sleek Japanese car with an Italian design, and it was only made in limited numbers for a short period of time. They're about as rare as hen's teeth—I dread to think how much it cost to import such a car into Panong.

Sarroch is leaning against it, casually, waiting for me.

"Is that supposed to impress me?"

"That's my car—I wasn't going to get a new one just for this evening, so whether you're impressed or not is beside the point."

Well, that puts paid any of Chai's ideas about this being a date. I don't think dates are supposed to start with an exchange of barbs, although it's been a while since I've been on one. I do have to admit that I'm impressed though—that's one hell of a beautiful car.

And Sarroch himself is looking pretty fine too. He's wearing the hasuta, the Panongian traditional dress for men. The top mirrors the pakay, closing diagonally across the chest, tucking into a wide sash that encircles the waist twice. The skirt is like a lighter and narrower version of the Japanese hakama.

Sarroch's hasuta is all in different tones of grey that complement the background of my pakay. Some men wear the hasuta awkwardly, but as Sarroch opens the car door for me, he moves with the athletic grace of someone used to it.

Once I'm settled in the car, I turn to him. "Now seriously, will you tell me what this is all about? I don't buy your excuse that we're going to be working more closely together.

Nor am I for one second going to believe that you've done such a one-eighty about me that you're suddenly craving my company."

Sarroch frowns. "At what point did I give you the impression that I was craving your company?"

"The pakay? The opera?"

"Yes. I tolerate your company enough that I'm willing to sit next to you in silence, in the dark, and watch what I consider to be one of the world's most amazing art form."

And that's put me right back in my box, not that I'd gone too far out of it. "Well, at least there's no chance of me getting a big head while in your company."

"You're Touched. There's not much for you to get bigheaded about."

I laugh. "Don't you know how to make a girl feel good of an evening."

Sarroch glances at me then back at the road. "You also look lovely."

"Oh. Um, thanks."

We lapse into an awkward silence. It was definitely better when he was insulting me.

* * *

Sarroch hadn't lied. Once we get to the opera we sit in silence, enjoying the performance, and then he drives me home. The conversation on the drive home is monosyllabic.

I still don't understand why he felt the need to buy me the pakay or take me to the opera, but sod it. I'm not too rich or too proud to pass up such an amazing gift as a hand-painted pakay.

It's a couple of days later, and life has somehow managed to settle back to normal, which sometimes feels surreal after recent events. I'm pottering in the house, getting ready to take Hunter out for a walk, when a knock comes at the door. I open to find the young, pretty couple who arrived all scared in the barbershop what feels like a lifetime ago.

"Oh, you're here!" I've summoned them using their tears in the extractor, but it's taken them an abnormally long time to answer. "I thought you would want to come and collect your youngling."

The girl's eyes are wide. "Can we see Zer?" Her voice trembles a little.

"Sure thing. This way." I lead the way. "Is 'Zer' your youngling's name?"

"Younglings don't have names for the first few years of their life," the beau replies. "They are simply Zer, until their form is fully established."

"Oh right, I see. And, um is Zer a boy or a girl?"

The female pari-pari smiles at me. "Which do you think?"

"Er..." I tried to get an anatomical read on the situation and the results were...confusing and unclear. But my gut tells me the youngling is female. "I think it's a girl"

"Well the truth is that younglings are neither and both. They are raw potential still to be realised and can go either way. When they finally settle into their final form, they also then settle into a single gender. But along the way they often play in one gender or the other, and if your intuition tells you Zer is female at the moment, you are probably right. For now."

The youngling sits on top of Fergie's shell, in the middle of my courtyard. Her weird straw-like hair is sticking out in all directions, and Barung, whose busted wing prevents him from flying, is standing on her head, patiently weaving her hair into something that looks like a nest.

"I've taken as good care of your youngling as I can, but it's probably a good thing you've come to take her away. I'm sure she's eager to be with her parents." Truth is, I have absolutely no idea how parent-youngling relationships work among the pari-pari.

The girl shakes her head. "She has chosen her environment, and it is not for us to move her. She seems happy here."

"Wait, what? You mean you're just leaving her with me? But I don't know the first thing about how to raise a pari-pari. I don't know what to feed her—so far she hasn't eaten anything that I've given her. She hasn't starved yet, but... and surely it's better for her to be with her own kind."

The girl threads her arm through her beau's, leaning against him. Her eyes are wide and sad, and I realise that they are shiny with tears. "We can't take her back. Not yet, anyway."

"But the pari-pari are no longer being hunted, right? And now that Zer is a youngling, she has no value to the Mayak anyway. No?"

The pari-pari don't answer, staring at their youngling.

I try a different tack. "Things are safe, now. Life can go back to normal for you."

The girl gives me a sad smile and shakes her head. There's pity in her eyes, and I suddenly feel about as wise as the toddlers I compare Mundanes to.

"Things haven't even truly begun yet," she says.

THE END FOR NOW

———

Most folks think being a supernatural barber is a quiet gig. Well, clearly, they've never had to play mediator between humans and the Mayak supernatural, with barely-there magic and a moody cat as backup.

Go to https://celinejeanjeanbooks.com/products/bound-by-silver to grab the next book in the series, Bound by Silver, and find out how Apiya gets on.

WANT MORE?

Want to find out how Apiya met Chai, how she met Mr Sangong and started working at the barbershop?

Join the newsletter to receive an ebook copy of Found by Rain, a prequel novella, for free.

Go to http://celinejeanjean.com/razor-bonus